A Kenyan Winterlude

THE NEW LANCASTER SERIES

A Kenyan Winterlude

The second novel of the New Lancastrian series

LORNA J. SHAW

authorHOUSE®

AuthorHouse™ LLC
1663 Liberty Drive
Bloomington, IN 47403
www.authorhouse.com
Phone: 1-800-839-8640

Published by AuthorHouse 02/05/2014

ISBN: 978-1-4918-6125-7 (sc)
ISBN: 978-1-4918-6126-4 (hc)
ISBN: 978-1-4918-6109-7 (e)

Library of Congress Control Number: 2014902225

I WOULD LIKE TO DEDICATE *this book to my two sons, John Dennie Shaw and Paul Edward Shaw for their unfailing love and patient technical support without which this book, and series would not be possible to have been written . . .*

"The African is conditioned by the culture and social institutions, of many centuries, to a freedom of which Europe has little conception, And it is not in his nature to accept serfdom forever . . . He realizes that He must fight unceasingly for his own emancipation; for without this, he is doomed to remain the prey of rival imperialisms."

Jomo Kenyatta (1891-1978) prime minister of Kenya1963 And President(1964-1978)

Chapter One

DOUGLAS PARKER TOOK OFF HIS reading glasses and rubbed his eyes. The electric clock on the wall behind his desk clicked monotonously as he looked out over the classroom of senior students, neat rows of quiet heads bent over their mid-term history examinations. Folding the morning's test papers from the freshman class, he stuffed them into his briefcase and rose to walk over to the rain-beaded window and stare at the sodden playing fields of New Lancaster Secondary School. The misty grey November afternoon, the lowering skies above the distant roof tops only added to the heaviness in his heart as he thrust his hands into his pockets and wondered when this dreadful feeling would go away. He turned and leaned against the window ledge to consider his class, promising bright young people whom he had nurtured through the early years and now faced a daily challenge of engaging them in the study and perceptions and evaluations of the human race in modern history.

The size of the senior class had shrunk dramatically from the swarms of freshmen who studied history, a required subject for the first year of school. He had always encouraged his students to examine the machinations of rulers and governments, the economics and follies of war, the explorations and migrations of peoples across the globe, but so many of the teen-agers opted for technical courses of carpentry, auto mechanics, word processing and computers. Their papers he had been marking all afternoon gave evidence to the lethargy of some of them to exercise their intellect not one iota past the bare minimum of effort. He could recognize the losers, the freeloaders all ready.

He walked slowly along the bank of windows to the back of the room and watched the drifting fog obliterate the top of the smoke stack at the lumber mill. Rotating his shoulders to relieve the muscular tension he stretched his neck to reach his height of almost six feet and leaned forward against the windowsill on strong hands accustomed to the rigours of sailing or the golf course. He gazed out again at the naked trees lining the street." Three more months of this place and then I'll be in Italy. God! I don't think I can wait that long."

His thoughts turned to Margaret Darwin, a woman whom he had met six months ago in the rain, her arms full of lilacs. He had fallen in love with her then but she had spurned his attempts toward a serious relationship. Two weeks ago she had been preparing to go on a vacation when their friendship came to an abrupt end in a sudden confrontation. He had lived in misery since. Now she was home again, back from the Bahamas, and he dreaded a chance meeting and the opening of old wounds.

"Only three more months and then it's off to Italy . . . But will I be able to forget her there? I've got to! I've got to get on with my life. But go on to what? What comes after Italy? What's left that makes any sense? I have to snap out of this depression. Maybe I should see the Doc and get some pills. Pills, booze . . . What's the difference? They're just crutches . . . I'm not going back to the booze. I'll get over this. Oh God! I can't go on like this" . . . He exhaled slowly, contemplating the lonely empty years of retirement looming aimlessly ahead.

The dismissal bell interrupted his despondent mood, and rubbing his hands together, he walked forward to his desk. "Okay. Let's wrap it up. How time flies when you're having fun . . ."

A basketball player in the front row disentangled his long legs and stood up. "Time flies like an arrow, Mr. Parker. Fruit flies like a banana," he said handing in his paper.

Doug frowned for a moment and then grinned. "You almost got me with that one, Gordon."

Several other students chuckled as they filed past his desk. Receiving the last paper, Doug snapped an elastic band around the sheaf, picked up his briefcase, turned off the lights and walked down the corridor to the office.

Susan, one of the secretaries, locked the papers in the safe room and said "By the way, Doug, here's a message for you. Jake took the call an hour or so ago."

He walked into the teachers' lounge and opened the note." Doug, Fiona MacPherson called. She wants you to stop by her house". He reached for his coat, wondering about the summons.

A cool mist drizzled onto the windshield as he drove over to Fiona's rooming house on Oak Terrace where Margaret lived and he hurried toward the porch to ring the bell . . . Inside, footsteps clumped down a flight of stairs and Ted, one of the resident college students, opened the door.

"Hi, Doug," he said. "How are yuh?"

"Fine, I guess. Is Fiona around?"

"No. She's working the evening shift."

"She left a message that she wanted me to stop by."

"Yeah. There's a letter for you in Margaret's room."

"Margaret's not here then?"

"No. Fiona said Margaret cut her vacation short in the Bahamas and went back to Toronto. She sent her suitcases home with Fiona though so she must be coming back soon. When Fiona arrived in Englewood last night, their luggage wasn't on the plane. The courier just delivered it this afternoon. I carried Margaret's bags down to her room and that's when we saw the letter for you. Do you want to go and get it?"

"Sure. I'll just be a minute."

Ted bounded upstairs as Doug walked down the hall and entered Margaret's room cautiously, unwilling to disturb those bittersweet memories of the woman he had loved and lost. The letter rested against the lamp beside her bed. Picking it up, he walked over to sit in her rocking chair by the bay window, tapping it gingerly, wondering. Then his finger lifted the flap.

My dearest Doug,

This is the only love letter I have written to anyone. I'm glad in a way because I can give you a first. A woman my age has so few left to offer. It is the last one too, because, by the time you read this, I will be in another place, and maybe another time. I say another time, darling, because I'm dying . . .

Doug stood up, his eyes transfixed.

Last spring I learned I have ovarian cancer, and coward that I am, I left Toronto and my family to spare them the inconvenience of the dying process. And so I came to New Lancaster, the loveliest little town this side of heaven. The loveliest, because it is the home of the man whom I love from the bottom of my heart.

Doug ran his fingers through his hair.

I respect you, Doug. I admire you. I believe you're the most wonderful, kindest man in the world. And you have so greatly honoured me with your love, a love I couldn't share. I love you too much, my darling, to allow you to suffer with me through the agony that will lie ahead.

Doug crumpled into her chair with tears streaming from his eyes. The words blurred on the page. I treasure every moment we have shared. I think I fell in love with you that first night you walked home with me from the beach. I'll carry those precious memories with me wherever I go.

I found another love in New Lancaster too, dearest Doug. I began a journey to find God and learned He was there all the time, waiting for me to want Him. Jesus is with me now, now and forever. And when I step into eternity, He will be there to take my hand.

Sobbing, Doug dropped the letter. "Why didn't you tell me? Why?" He pulled out his handkerchief and muffled the sounds of his anguish. Wiping his eyes at last, he picked up the letter.

I wish things were different. I don't want to die. But if this hadn't happened, I'd have never met you, and maybe I wouldn't have been moved to meet Jesus either. I know I've hurt you with my seeming indifference to your love. You'll never know how close I was to giving myself to you the night of the Fair. Please believe me, darling. Your grief would be far greater now if I had.

He rose to walk about her room, breathing deeply to relieve the enormous pain in his chest.

You were so angry the last time I saw you. Will you forgive me for the mess I've made of your life? And don't leave New Lancaster. I'll become a memory, not a ghost . . . And when you're sailing some summer day, look up at the blue sky and tell me you love me still. And when you feel a raindrop on your cheek it's only me saying I miss you.

Goodbye, Douglas James Parker. I pray that you will find the peace that passes understanding, the peace that only God can give to you as He has given it to me.

M.

He threw himself down on the bed and wept into her pillow. Her face lay beside him. If only you'd told me . . . We could have been together for a little while. Anything would be better than this awful loneliness. He turned over at last and caught sight of a row of suitcases beside the wall. Pushing himself off the bed, he opened the closet door to find it empty. The drawers in the bureau were empty too. Where are you? Where did you go.? . . .

He went over to sit by the window again with his head in his hands. You'll want your clothes . . . You'll send for them and when you do . . .

He picked up the letter and read it through over and over again weeping softly and desperately trying to draw comfort from her words of love. Wiping his eyes at last, he carried all her bags out to his car, came back into the quiet house once more to look around her room, smoothing the rumpled covers on her bed. "You'll never leave me again," he said softly and closed the door.

As Doug got out of the car in his garage, Hobo, the wire-haired terrier from next door, danced about his feet, bouncing an old tennis ball. He leaned down to ruffle the dog's neck. "Not tonight, boy." He tossed the ball out onto the lawn and closed the garage door.

His weekly cleaning woman, Mrs. Clark, had already gone and he could smell his supper cooking in the oven. Turning off the gas, he went into the bedroom intending to change his clothes, but too weary to bother, he slumped down onto the chaise instead. Staring dispiritedly at the dusk settling over the neighbourhood, he heard Hobo barking at squirrels and then remembered the Wilsons, next door, had gone away and the dog was to stay with him for the night. Unable to shrug off his lethargy, Doug lay back and gazed numbly at the ceiling.

His bedroom was a pleasant place now. After Janet died, he thought he would never sleep in it again. Almost three years ago, he had come home from school one afternoon and found his wife lying on their bed, her head in a mass of congealed blood from a ruptured aneurysm in her brain. Grief-stricken, he and his son and daughter had endured the formal period of bereavement, and Doug had continued to sleep in the other bed in Michael's room after Michael returned home to Nairobi, and Anne had gone back to Toronto. When Anne came home at Christmas, she was surprised to see her father still sleeping in the twin bed in the cramped room.

"Come on, Dad. It's time to move on."

"I can't sleep in that room. I see your mother every time I go in there."

"Then let me fix it up . . . Change it. I'll get rid of the bed and move the furniture."

"You don't need to bother . . ."

"Yes I do. It's hard enough to lose Mother. I don't want to lose you too."

"You're not going to lose me."

"Look. You're all I've got left, with Michael so far away. You're changing, Dad. You drink too much and you're becoming like a shell. You've got to get out and live again. Mother's gone! I miss her, and I know you do too, even more than I do, but we've got to get on with our lives."

He relented to her earnest pleas, and before she returned to Toronto after the New Year, she had redecorated the room. He had helped her strip off the flowered paper, and paint the walls a soft blue. The double bed had been replaced by a queen size mattress. "No one sleeps in a double bed any more, Dad." She bought a striped white and blue denim comforter, navy sheets and a matching skirt for the box spring. The chaise had been sent to the upholsterer to be covered in the same denim stripe, and she had moved her own desk into the corner exchanging it for her mother's dressing table. Navy drapes replaced the white frilly curtains. She had even hung different pictures on the walls, prints of sailboats.

Doug listened to the north wind whistling through the pines at the corner of the house. I thought I'd reached the bottom of the pit when I lost you, Janet. The loneliness . . . . I couldn't bear to come home after school to the empty house. I'd drive up to the cemetery and sit by your grave and talk to you. And one day, Deirdre saw me there. She'd come to put a wreath on her father's grave. You'd have laughed at her, Janet. She almost looked like you when she said, "Douglas! This is unhealthy!" And it was. I stopped going to see you after that. I'd drive by once in a while but I had to let you go. I'm sorry we didn't have time to say goodbye.

Well I sure said goodbye to Margaret, didn't I. But now, I can't let her go. Not this way. Oh Janet . . . I remember telling her the way I lost you was easier than the way she lost her husband. What did I say . . . Something about watching someone you love, die slowly . . . I wonder if that's why she couldn't tell me.?

He began to cry and rose quickly to go into the bathroom to splash cold water on his face. I should call Fiona at work and ask if she's heard from her. No. Not tonight. I'm in no shape to talk to anybody tonight.

Pulling on his terry bathrobe, he went out to get the letter from his jacket, opened the front door and whistled loudly. Hobo scampered inside, and when Doug went into the living room and slouched in his chair in the corner, the little dog wriggled up into his lap. Waves were roaring out of a black night along the rocky breakwater at the end of the lawn, crashing into the pier across the river. Sitting in the shadows, Doug rubbed the dog's ears distractedly and held her precious letter against his cheek.

Hungry and impatient for supper, Hobo finally jumped down and went out to the kitchen to push his dog dish about in the corner. Sighing, Doug heaved himself to his feet to fill the bowl with dog food, then went into the bedroom to finish marking the freshman examination papers. Hobo padded in and curled up in his basket beside the desk. Forcing himself to concentrate on his work, Doug finished the last paper at midnight and was recording the marks in his ledger when the telephone rang. Hobo raised his head. Doug stared at it for a moment and then picked up the receiver.

"Doug? It's Fiona. Did I wake you?"

"No."

"You got the letter?"

"Yes."

"I thought you might like to know there was a message from Margaret on my machine when I got home from work a few minutes ago."

He held his breath.

"Are you there?"

"Yes."

"She asked me to leave the door open tonight because she doesn't have her keys and she's coming in on the early train."

His heart stopped.

"Doug? Did you hear me?"

"Yes."

"Okay. I just thought you'd like to know . . ."

He closed his eyes. "Thanks for calling, Fiona."

He hung up the receiver and sat numbly on the chair. She's coming back. Oh God! She's coming back! What will I do? What will I say? He dreaded facing her and the awful truth, sharing her terrible grief. The anticipated thrill of seeing her again was overshadowed by the agony of losing another love. He rose to pace about the room, weeping and wondering if it was truly better to have loved and lost than to never have loved at all. "Oh God! Help me. Help us!"

He went into the bathroom to splash more cold water on his puffy eyes. His wiry hair stood in disarray. The wrinkles at the corners of his blue eyes seemed deeper; his weathered face, sallow: his chin, shadowed and grey. He sighed and reached for his shaving cream. By the time he stepped out of a hot shower he knew exactly what he would do.

New Lancaster lay in sleepy silence as Doug pulled into the empty parking lot at the darkened station. The clock on the dash told him he had twenty minutes to wait, and sitting under the lonely yardlight, he mindlessly watched the ice crystals swirling along the platform. The car grew colder as the north wind blasted down from the desolate plain but he didn't notice. His senses were honed to wait for the diesel horn at the crossing at the south end of town. At last he heard the forlorn wail, and swinging himself out of the seat, drew a big breath. "Be strong. She's going to need you."

The engine glided past the station and came to a halt further along the platform from where he stood waiting in the shelter from the wind. He watched her step down from the car, her hair shining in the lighted doorway. An older man assisted her down the last step and took her elbow as they walked briskly toward the station. He caught his breath. She drew near and he stepped from the shadows, his arm outstretched as if to bar her way. "Margaret . . ."

She turned toward him, her face breaking into a smile. "Doug . . ." She stepped into the open circle and kissed his cheek.

"I got your letter . . ."

She kissed his cheek again.

He put his other arm around her. "I love you . . ." His voice quavered and he knew he was going to cry. "Won't you trust me to love you all the way?"

She tilted her head back to see his eyes filled with tears and clasped his face in her hands. "I'm not dying, Doug. It was all a terrible mistake. I saw the doctor this afternoon and I'm going to live to be a hundred."

His fragile grief shattered and he felt himself falling apart in her arms. Clinging to her he poured out the anguish of the past agonizing hours and sobbed into the fragrance of her hair. She stroked the back of his neck. "It's all right, darling. It's all right."

His mind was racing, faltering, falling.

"I love you so much," she whispered, her lips brushing his ear, his cheek.

He hugged her fiercely, kissing her hungrily, starving for her love.

She drew away from him breathlessly and smiled into his eyes. "Take me home now. I have so much to tell you. So much more to share." She turned to their audience of one.

"Doug, this is Peter Spencer, a friend of Harry Copse. Can we give him a lift over to the rectory?"

Doug squared his shoulders and held out his hand. "Of course we can do that right away."

\ Peter Spencer said, "I think I'll take a stroll because it's obvious that you two have some catching up to do. And you won't want me around. I'll look for a taxi."

She stooped to pick up her shoulder bag and he caught her around the waist to sweep her across the platform into the waiting car. She was shivering violently as he opened the door to climb in behind the wheel and her teeth chattered, "I'm soooo cold."

He turned the key in the ignition before reaching out to draw her close, breathing her name. She traced kisses across his cheek, seeking his lips with an unfamiliar passion, and when his mouth found hers, the intensity of the consummation convinced her that love was indeed lovelier the second time around.

The train pulled out of the station. Doug put his arm around her and kissed her again. "Are you all right, dear?" The car started rolling across the parking lot.

She lay her hand on his knee. "Yes."

"Are you really all right? What did the doctor say? What happened?"

"It's such a long story . . . After John died, I was feeling rotten. Stomach-aches. Tired all the time. Depressed. And so I went to this new clinic because our old family doctor had left town . . . After several tests, the doctor called in a specialist. I had more blood tests and the lab report indicated that I had an advanced case of ovarian cancer with a very poor prognosis. They wanted to operate on me right away and I was willing, at first . . . But then, I started thinking about the quality of my life with all the radiation and chemo-therapy afterwards. I just couldn't face all the uncertainty, the loss of control over my physical condition, the new experimental treatments they were sure to use on me. Anyway, I decided not to go through with it after all. And that's when I came to New Lancaster . . ."

Doug drew her closer. "And I met you."

She stroked his knee. "In the Bahamas I got really sick . . . And on the way home this big lump in my abdomen suddenly ruptured."

"My God!" The car swerved slightly and he steadied the wheel. "Margaret!"

"I went back to the clinic and that's when Dr. Green discovered that the lab had made a mistake. They got my report mixed up with another woman's. She died two months ago and I got the reprieve." She turned to kiss Doug's cheek. "After that, all I could think of was you, darling. I wanted to rush home and tell you the good news."

With one hand he maneuvered the car around the corner of the station . . . "So the lab got the tests mixed up . . ."

"Yes."

"And the doctor is quite sure about you?"

"Yes. He thinks it was an ovarian cyst."

"He thinks! Doesn't he know?"

"He'll know more after getting the results of the tests he did today. I'll call him next Tuesday. The specialist will probably do some more tests too."

"I'll take you to Toronto, Margaret. I want to meet this Doctor Green. Couldn't he see you weren't dying? Is he competent? Or negligent . . ."

She shook her head. "You didn't know me then, Doug. I was a wreck. And the doctor said if I'd had the surgery they'd have discovered the mistake then. So it was my fault too."

"The other woman, the one who died . . . If her family knew about this, they'd be calling their lawyer."

Margaret drew away from Doug and turned to face him. "It wouldn't have helped her either. By then she was so full of cancer that she didn't have a chance. I don't want to even think of pursuing this. Dr. Green is an excellent doctor. He's very caring and kind. None of this was his fault. If the staff in the hematology lab worry about a lawsuit from the other family it might keep them on their toes." She reached out to touch his cheek. "I'm just thankful to be still alive and here with you." She looked up and saw Peter Spencer shivering at the corner of the building . . . "Oh Doug, we should give the poor man a ride now."

"Off course", he pulled up to the corner of the building and got out of the car. Margaret heard him introduce himself again and

Peter Spencer replied, "So you're the fellow Margaret's been praying about."

Doug grinned "I hope so."

.Peter rubbed his chin. "I told her 'Better to marry than burn.'

Doug frowned "Why burn in hell for what? Sex?"

Peter shook his head. "No, no. You've got the wrong idea. St. Paul was talking about burning with lust."

Doug opened the back door and said,.", Peter, We'll run you over to Harry's before you freeze."

Peter said "Thanks and do you two want to marry?"

Margaret turned around to look at Peter and said," But I can't marry Doug until he asks me."

Doug held up his hands." Okay! okay, Margaret, my darling, will you marry me?"

Margaret smiled, "I thought you'd never ask.".

Peter Spencer clapped his hands, "I can't wait to see Harry's face when I tell him he's got a wedding to perform before we go to bed."

Doug squeezed Margaret's hand. "Peter, do you usually drag people in from the street to be married?"

Peter Spencer laughed, "Only in very special cases, and that's you. two."

Doug stopped the car in the driveway at twelve Pearl Street. As Peter went into the house, Margaret wrapped her arms around Doug and whispered, "Can you believe this?"

He kissed her forehead and said, "I can and I wonder what he's telling Harry Copse."

"Here they come, Peter probably thinks we're members of Harry's congregation,", she said as the two priests left the house and motioned to them to follow across the street.

Doug squeezed her hand and said "If what I hear about Harry Copse is true, the poor man won't even know the difference. He's having trouble unlocking the door."

Harry reached for the switch, and the sanctuary was ablaze with light . . . Margaret took off her coat and shivered. "I'm going to wear my coat through the ceremony. It's cold in here"

Doug took off his hat and hung it on the nearest pew. And so they were married repeating their vows before a sleepy old rector wearing a worn parka with a moth eaten,fur trimmed hood, and Peter, bundled up in a shabby overcoat with a wool scarf wrapped around his scrawny neck.

. Doug substituted a wedding band with a school insignia ring which had arrived that morning in the principal' s office as a special gift from the senior class for their mentor . . .

Margaret stretched out her hand as they proceeded into Harry's office to sign the register., "I'll wear the ring on my thumb, dear, so I don't lose it."

"Please don't. It was a gift from the senior class, so it's very special."

After saying goodbye to the priests, they were reminded to buy a license early in the morning so Harry could sign it before he left for Ottawa.

With one hand on the steering wheel and his other arm around his bride, Doug navigated his way around the corner onto Oak Terrace.

Glancing at the darkened house sleeping in the silent night, Margaret remembered other times he had driven her home and she had discouraged his advances. Now she turned to look into his face, a solemn mask in the shadows.

He kissed her fingers. "When I went to meet the train tonight my only thought was to hold you in my arms and take care of you for the rest of your life. But now, everything's changed . . . I'll take care of you for the rest of my life."

She moistened her lips. "I love you, Doug . . . I've missed all those feelings of being loved, . . . My arms have been empty for such a long long time. When we danced that night at the Fair, I had to force my feet to walk away from you because I wanted you so badly." She reached out and touched his cheek. "Let me hold you for the rest of my life. So you can take me home, I'm your wife now and I'll love you forever."

He sighed deeply and drew her close again. As she kissed his neck, he managed to steer the car into the street and drive the rest of the way down Oak Terrace on wheels two feet off the ground.

The garage doors closed slowly behind them. As he climbed out of the car, she slid behind the wheel and stepped up into his arms. He brought her into his home for the first time and she glanced about the orderly kitchen; the drawn shades covering a row of windows above the opposite counter and sink; the gleaming appliances; a pantry and utility room opening off one end of the galley; a round oaken table and chairs at the other end of the room in front of a wide glass door;

a hanging lamp over the table casting a soft glow into the shadows beyond.

She heard the jingling sound of dog tags and Hobo ran into the kitchen as Doug draped his coat over a stepstool by the door. "Hey, boy. We've got company. Margaret's come to stay."

She stooped down to pat the dog's head for a moment.

When he reached for her coat she straightened up and sniffed. "What have you been cooking? It smells delicious."

He walked over to lay her coat across the table. "It's Mrs. Clark's pot pie. She comes in once a week to clean up after me and makes my supper."

Margaret slipped off her shoes, walked toward him and wrapped her arms around his neck. "And now you won't need Mrs. Clark because I'll be here to take care of you."

He drew her close, molding her body as their lips brushed. Her fingers clasped the back of his head pressing his mouth against her lips. Electrifying sensations intensified as he embraced her more tightly and she opened her mouth slightly, trembling as he kissed her deeply, urgently.

She turned her head slightly. "Do you want to, darling?"

He groaned softly, "Oh Margaret . . ."

She stretched her body closer and kissed him again . . .

He put his arm around her waist and led her across the foyer down a hall into his room where a lamp shone on the night table. She glanced at the bed for a moment as he fumbled with the buttons on her blouse. Clumsily, she tried to unbutton his shirt too and their arms became entangled. They laughed together nervously and hastily undressed themselves.

Stepping out of his slacks, Doug threw back the bedcovers and sat down on the chaise in his shorts to take off his socks and shoes. Margaret folded her skirt over the desk chair and sat down on the side of the bed to remove her pantyhose. He came to her then, clasping her shoulders, kissing her gently, pushing her back into the middle of the bed. She lay quietly, her hair, an aura in the pool of lamplight, her satin and lace slip very white against the darkblue sheets, her green eyes luminous, watching intently his every move. He slid onto the bed beside her, propping himself on his elbow and began to caress the satin and lace.

A thump on the end of the bed distracted them and they looked down to see Hobo standing on the comforter, watching, . . . Doug smiled and rose to scoop the dog up into his arm. "Not tonight, fella. Three's a crowd." He set the dog out in the hall and closed the door.

Hobo stared at the door, cocking his head to the slight sounds in the house. The pine trees were brushing against the eaves and he trotted into the cool, dark living room, his dog tags jingling in the shadows. He jumped up on a chair and looked out the black window where an icy wind thrashed the glass. The room seemed lonely without the man, and he jumped down to search his bowl for a last morsel. The woman's coat hung down over the edge of the table and he sniffed at the unfamiliar scent as he lay down under the table in another resting place, his favourite because the man sat here to read the paper in the morning and fed him crusts of toast. Now the floor was cold and bare. He walked slowly up the hall and pushed on the bedroom door with his nose. The latch gave way and he crept into his warm basket and heard the woman sigh, "Was it ever this wonderful?"

The man said, "I'm glad the Wilson's are away. Those bells and fireworks probably woke up the rest of the neighbourhood."

"Are you always this funny?"

"What do you mean? Didn't you hear them too?"

She stirred in his arms and laughed softly.

He lay back on his pillow. "What a way to start the day!"

She yawned. "Or end one."

He looked at his watch. "We'd better get some sleep "We've got a busy day ahead of us. He swung him\self out of bed and pulled on his shorts to go into the bathroom. She heard him brushing his teeth.

Slipping out of bed, she went into the bathroom too. "Could I borrow a toothbrush?"

He rinsed his brush under the tap. "What is it you Anglicans say when you marry? Something about 'with all my worldly goods I thee endow'?" He presented her with his brush and opened the door of the medicine chest over the sink. "Everything I have is yours, my love . . ." He kissed the tip of her nose and left her to her ablutions.

When she went back into the bedroom he was waiting for her, his chest bare against the sheets. She reached toward the lamp.

"Don't turn it off, darling. I want to watch you undress."

"No you don't," she said. "I'm not twenty any more."

"Neither am I. But it doesn't matter."

She slipped her straps over her shoulders, and unfastened her bra. Dropping the satin and lace on the floor, she climbed into bed beside him, and feeling the curly hairs of his body soft against her skin, she murmured, "With my body, I thee worship."

He reached over to turn out the light, and cradling her in his arms, he finally felt her relaxing into sleep, breathing gently against his neck.

The ringing of the telephone awoke them "Who on earth could that be at this hour of the morning?".

Doug cleared his throat. "It's probably the neighbours complaining about the racket over here last night." He hesitated "Hello?"

"Doug? It's Fiona. I just woke up and Margaret's not here Have you seen her? Did you meet the train? I wonder where she could have gone. Perhaps I should call Walt and see if he has taken her some place."

Doug smiled "You don't have to worry about her. I met her at the train and brought her here. Would you like to speak with her?" He handed the phone to Margaret and crawled over top of her so the cord wouldn't strangle him.

She hesitated "Fiona? Are you just getting home now?"

"No" Fiona replied "We had a very busy night in the emergency room. Two women rushed in to deliver babies before they were even admitted. Then Harry Copse came in with a friend and died. of a heart attack That was a shock. His poor friend didn't know what to do so we called the coroner and the undertaker. It seems Harry was supposed to drive to Ottawa today. He might have died on the way, so it's good it happened while he was still here at home. I guess they're making arrangements for him to leave on the ten o'clock train. this morning. By the way, Margaret what are you and Doug doing at this time of night?"

"We have a lot to talk about and it may take all night. I'll get back to you later". She handed the receiver back to Doug and told him about Harry Copse' demise. "Could we change sides again? This doesn't feel right." She climbed over top of Doug and they lay quietly musing the turn of events of the last few hours. "Poor old Harry" she said. "After the Midge and Brian fiasco, I I thought he'd never perform another marriage ceremony and now as it turns out, our wedding was his last."

Doug hugged her. "I'm awfully glad he did."

The snuggled contentedly in the warm bed listening to the pelting rain on the side of the house . . . They made love slowly savouring each touch and nuance of their passion and after they both had reached an ecstatic climax she clung to him fiercely, crying "Oh, don't ever let me go!. "He held her and stroked her brow until they both drowsed into a contented sleep.

Later, Margaret awoke to the sound of a voice, and for a moment, wondered where she was, in a darkened room with a streak of daylight peeping through a crack in the drapes. "Jake? It's Doug . . . I won't be in today . . . No. Something's come up. You'll have to get someone to cover for me . . . I may not be in tomorrow either, but I'll be back for classes on Thursday, for sure . . . Yes . . . Okay. Thanks."

She listened to the sounds of running water, cabinet doors opening and closing, then a long silence and the rustling of paper. When she smelled smoke she realized he was lighting a fire in the fireplace. He came into the room, and in the dim light, she watched him taking off his robe and slipping back into bed.

"Good morning," she said softly.

He moved closer to her. "You're awake . . ."

"You're cold," she said, touching his feet.

"I should have turned up the thermostat last night," he said. "I don't mind it chilly for sleeping, but the wind's out of the north-east this morning and all the glass on that side of the house makes it really cold. I closed the drapes and lit a fire so that should help to warm it up."

She tucked the blanket under his chin. "I like to sleep in a cold room too."

He turned on his side and propped his head on his hand. "We have a lot to learn about each other, don't we."

"I have no complaints so far. But I noticed you roll the tooth paste and I squeeze."

"Oh dear," he sighed. "I guess I shouldn't marry you after all."

"Not a chance," she giggled. "You've made an honest woman out of me . . . You can't wriggle out of this Douglas Parker."

He pulled her close to him. "And I don't want to either."

The aroma of fresh coffee eventually drifted into the bedroom. "Would Madam prefer her breakfast in bed this morning?" he asked.

"If you can find Madam something to wear then she'll arise."

He laughed and reached for his old terry robe. "One of the good things about having a grown daughter is that she buys me clothes for

Christmas I never wear." He went over to the bureau and brought out a new green tartan dressing gown. "Just for you, Madam."

She laughed and got out of bed.

They ate a leisurely breakfast and carried their coffee into the living room to sit on the sofa in front of the crackling logs behind the glass doors on the hearth. Margaret shivered as she watched the angry lake whipping waves high onto the rocks along the shore. Doug put his arm around her and propped his feet on the coffee table.

"Does your mother know you put your feet on the furniture?" she asked.

"I don't think so. Does it matter?"

Margaret stroked his bare foot with her toe. "No. You'd probably do it anyway." She turned her head. "Some day you'll have to tell me about your mother, and the rest of your family. Do you have any brothers or sisters?"

"No. My only sister died five years ago. And my parents died long before that. You'll have to tell me about your family too . . . But now I want to hear about your trip to the Bahamas. Did you have a good time?"

She bit her lip. "No. It was awful. I never want to go there again."

He drew his arm away and sat up straight. "What happened?"

She sighed. "I know this will be hard for you to believe but since I last saw you, darling, I've been in a plane crash and marooned on an island. I stowed away on a scow loaded with cocaine, almost drowned in the ocean, blew up two boats, put three men in the hospital, broke into some poor woman's house and helped myself to her larder, hitch-hiked into Freeport and flew home looking like Medusa."

He stood up and stared at her. "Who?"

"Oh, I forgot you don't know your poetry. Medusa was one of the Gorgons in Greek mythology. She had a horrible face and had snakes coming out of her hair. Anyone who saw her turned to stone until Perseus cut off her head."

"Margaret!"

"You should have seen me, Doug. I'd have turned you to stone too."

"What on earth are you talking about? Plane crashes! Blowing up boats! Have you gone crazy?"

She stood and walked over to the window. "Maybe . . . Sometimes I wonder."

He frowned.

"I think I have POTSS . . ."

He lowered his brow and chin. "Pots! What in the world are you talking about!"

"Post Trauma Stress Syndrome . . ."

He shook his head.

She realized she was clenching her fists, and shoved them in the pockets of the dressing gown to hide them from his view. "It was awful, Doug . . ." She turned to look out the window.

He stared at her back for a long moment wondering what this was all about and sat down slowly on the sofa.

She turned to see him watching her. "We all learn to cope with stress one way or another sometime in our lives . . . I thought I'd reached my limit with John, and then all that business with Jane and my sons, but . . ."

Doug raised his eyebrows and was about to ask about "all that business" when he sensed she had something she needed to say and needed to say it very badly. He walked over to put his arm around her. "Let's sit down, dearest. Tell me all about it."

She sat stiffly on the edge of the sofa so he perched on the coffee table and took both of her hands. "Now what's wrong?"

"I shouldn't have gone to the Bahamas," she began. "I was such a wreck emotionally because I knew I was leaving you forever . . . And I felt terrible physically. My side was aching continually and the tumour was growing bigger every day . . . But everyone in town was saying 'Goodbye' and 'Have a nice trip', and Fiona was awfully excited, so I had to go.

"After we got there, the pain grew worse. l started to feel bloated all the time, and that scared me."

"What did Fiona say?"

"She didn't know about it. She'd met a man, a theatrical agent from Toronto, and they were having fun together and I told her it was the Bahamian food that was making me sick and I'd be all right."

He frowned. "Wasn't there a hospital or some place you could have gone?"

"There was a government clinic, but I didn't think they could help me without really getting into a lot of tests and x-rays and they probably didn't have the equipment . . . Anyway, I finally realized I just had to go home. But when I tried to get a flight out of Georgetown to Freeport, I learned Bahamasair was already overbooked and so there I was, stuck in this little tin shack."

"A shack!"

"Our reservations got mixed up but that's another story. Anyway, early one morning, a seaplane landed out front. The pilot was having engine trouble and I lent him my moped to go to the airport to get a new fuel pump. When he returned later that afternoon, he said he hoped he'd make it to Freeport before morning. I asked if I could get a ride with him but he refused, to take a passenger saying, it was something to do with his license and insurance. Little did I know the real reason he didn't want me aboard was because he was carrying a load of cocaine."

"Cocaine!" Doug gaped at her.

"Yes. There must have been at least a ton of it. Anyway, that night after he fixed the engine and took the lantern back to the bartender at the Mermaid, I sneaked on board and stowed away back in the tail."

"Margaret!" He clapped his hands on his cheeks.

"I'd written a note to Fiona telling her I was going home but couldn't take my luggage with me so she'd have to take care of it."

He shook his head in disbelief . . .

"We took off very early in the morning. I guess he had to wait for the tide. Anyway, it was awful. The plane was bouncing so hard on the water, I thought I'd die. And just when I couldn't stand it any more, we finally came off and I collapsed on an old tarpaulin at the back behind the pile of cargo. The pilot was talking to someone on a radio . . . And then after a while, one of the engines sputtered and quit. He got on the radio again, told them where he was and said he was going to have to set it down near Hog's Cay."

She stood up and walked over to the window again. "And then, while he was still talking, the other engine stopped too. There was this deadly silence before the plane started to fall. The pilot began screaming, 'Mayday! Mayday!' I stood up and screamed too. I saw the water rushing up, or us rushing down . . . And then everything went black."

She began to pace frantically in front of the window and Doug knit his brows wondering if he should intervene.

"I slowly regained consciousness lying half submerged in water in the tail section of the plane. It seemed like it was a bad dream . . . The tiny lights on the ceiling in the front part of the cabin, and the panel lights in the cockpit were still glowing under water but it was quite dark. I could see the cargo had been flung everywhere. When I finally realized what had happened, that the pilot must be dead down below in the cockpit . . . I think I went crazy then, Doug. I knew it was only a matter of time before I would be dead too. There was so little space, so little air. I began to scream . . ."

She covered her ears. "Those screams still echo in my head . . . And then I remembered the letter and telling you that Jesus would be with me when I died . . . So I cried out for Him to help me die. I was so scared . . ."

Her voice broke. Doug rose and came to hold her close.

"Then I remembered what one of the men over at First Baptist had said when Jack Ferguson was so ill in the hospital. He read to us from the Bible 'When you pass through the waters, I will be with you' . . . That seemed to comfort me and I finally lay back quietly waiting to die and see Jesus . . .

"But then I heard waves lapping against the hull and I realized the tail must be sticking out of the water and if I could only get the hatch open and get outside then I could hang on to something and wait to be rescued."

He stroked her back.

"My shoulders were so sore I could hardly move. I honestly don't know how I did it but finally, I opened the hatch and swam up into the dark sea."

"Oh Margaret . . ."

"I could see the tail in the moonlight and found a wire there to hold onto."

"And . . ."

"And so I waited, hanging onto the wire, drifting until dawn."

"When did you find out about the cocaine?"

"Later that morning. More of the fuselage became visible with the ebbing tide and I was able to sit on the edge of the hatch, still sure I would be rescued. But then the tide changed and I knew I had to find a life jacket or something because I was too weak to hold onto the wire for another six hours. I knew I'd drown for sure. And so I wondered about the cargo. Perhaps there was something inside the plane I could use. I reached down for a loose bundle and stabbed the plastic cover with my keys. When white powder floated away on the water I knew the only people who would come looking for the plane were the drug dealers."

He led her back to the sofa and sat down holding her in his arms. She stared into the fire. "You may not believe this, Doug, but I know God was there with me, helping me, showing me what to do. There was a small mangrove island with a little sandy beach not too far away, and I managed to swim to it. I found an old coconut with some milk inside, and a garbage bag . . . I was out of my mind sometimes because I was in shock from the crash . . . Just staying alive for the next hour, the next minute, was all I could handle. For a long time I didn't even feel the severity of the pain in my stomach and shoulders . . . I remember feeling terrified and completely hopeless . . . I knew that I would die eventually, all alone, that no one would ever know what happened to me. My bones would lie there on the sand, bleached white by the sun after the crabs had finished . . ."

She shuddered violently and he held her close.

"And then God sent the rain, wonderful life-giving rain. I started to think rationally after that . . . Dying didn't seem to matter anymore. I had made my peace with God and I resigned myself to the fact that I would die. I sat there under the mangroves waiting and thinking, thinking about Jesus and all the things He did, remembering the Bible verses and the hymns we sing in church. I didn't actually hear His voice but now I realize He was speaking to me all the time through those words.

"And then the drug dealers came on an old tug in the middle of the night. God helped me swim back to the wreck and climb on their boat while they were getting the cocaine out of the plane. He gave me a hiding place under a lifeboat on top of the wheelhouse and I found some crackers and cheese and oranges and even a can of beer."

He shifted his arm. "I thought you didn't like beer, darling."

"I don't but it was the only thing I could find to drink. Drug dealers don't drink tea, Doug. I hid on that boat all day and most of the next night. And then a speedboat rendezvoused near an island. Before they started to unload the cocaine, I got out from under the lifeboat, set fire to the scow with some matches I had found, and jumped overboard."

"My God!"

"I nearly drowned at first in the huge swells but it was almost worth it when I watched millions of dollars of cocaine go up in flames.

Fortunately the tide carried me in but it was still a long swim and it was dark, so awfully dark with only the sound of the surf to tell me where I was . . . And there was an undertow that almost finished me . . . When I finally got on shore I just collapsed . . . Next morning I found a little house where there was food and water and I managed to pull myself together for the trip home."

"My God! I can hardly believe this."

"Neither can I."

"Well you're home now," he said, pulling her closer. "Safe and sound."

"Not so sound," she said, staring at the embers. "The horror of it all came back to me on the plane to Toronto. I held pillows over my ears trying to block out the sound of the engines because I was terrified that they would stop and the plane would start to fall . . ." She shivered. "And after I got to a hotel, I had terrible nightmares . . . The last one was the worst because you were with me in the ocean and we were both drowning and I couldn't reach you . . ." Tears flowed down her cheeks as she remembered her dreams. "I woke up crying, `I want to live. Oh God! Let us live!' That's when I realized how precious life is . . . That's when I decided to go back to the doctor and do everything possible to stay alive. And you know the rest of the story."

He wiped the tears from her eyes.

"I'm still afraid, Doug. I don't want to remember it again. Even as I was telling you about it now, I felt the terror of being trapped in that tiny space in the tail . . . I'll never get in another little plane as long as I live. And I can't bear crowded elevators . . . Living all alone, dying alone . . ." She shuddered. "Oh hold me close."

He wrapped his arms around her and she lay against him, listening to the grandfather clock chiming in the hall, the wind beating against the glass panes. "Do you think I should go to see a shrink?" she said at last.

He stroked her hair. "I don't know. You've certainly been through a bad time . . . But you said God helped you. Maybe you could talk to Angus, or Jack Ferguson . . ."

She twisted herself around to face him. "I've been thinking that maybe I shouldn't tell anyone else about this. It might be better to keep it just between us."

He brushed the hair from her forehead. "All right."

They lay together on the sofa in a contented silence as the rain pelted the windows and the room grew cold. Doug rose to build up the fire and came back to look down at her. The telephone rang. And Doug whispered as he picked up the receiver "It's probably another one of the neighbours complaining about the fireworks last night "He answered, "Hello?"

"It's Fiona, Doug. Is Margaret still there?"

"Yes, she's right here. He carried the phone into the living room, a long cord trailing

"How about if I call Angus and make an appointment for him to marry us again properly ?"

She reached for his hand and pulled him down to the sofa. "Do we have to do it today?"

"You do want to marry me in a regular ceremony to feel married. I didn't understand much of it last night"

"Yes, it's so good just being here with you, and the weather's awful, and we'll need witnesses. I feel like I'm home now after a long journey, like I'm safe at last. You're my refuge, Doug . . . And I don't want to share our happiness with anyone else just yet."

"So what do you want to do?"

She smiled. "I just want to stay here and watch the fire and the rain, and make love again and again . . ."

"Hey. Wait a minute. I told you I'm not twenty years old, didn't I?"

She giggled. "All right. We'll concentrate on the quality instead of quantity."

He kissed her forehead. "I never dreamed that you would be so wonderful. You're the most interesting woman in the whole world and I'm going to love every moment of the rest of our lives together."

"Don't you think we might have a quarrel once in a while?"

"I think even fighting with you will be fun, and making up after will be even better."

She yawned and stood up. "How about another cup of coffee? I think I'd like to go back to bed for awhile.\

Doug smiled "What a good idea It's Fiona. She wants to talk to you"

Margaret hesitated. "Fiona?"

"

"Hey !Margaret! What are you doing at Doug's this time of the morning?"

She smiled at Doug. "We're planning our wedding."

"Your wedding!"

She sat on the arm of the sofa. "Look Fiona. It's a long story, and don't breathe a word of this to anyone yet, but Doug and I are getting married just as soon as we can and I want you to be my bridesmaid."

Doug leaned toward the telephone "And I'm asking Ed to be my bridesmaid . . . ."

.Fiona laughed, "Well this is really something . . . So I'm losing my gardener."

Margaret smiled, "Yes. Doug's offered me a good job with more pay and better benefits."

"And I can never match those benefits. Are you sure you're doing the right thing?"

Margaret looked up at Doug who was puzzled by the conversation. "I've never been more sure of anything in my whole life. Please Fiona, don't mention a word of this to anyone We want to keep it a secret until it's all over I'll get back to you when we know what we're doing."

"Okay" Fiona said "And I'm really happy for both of you. Goodbye."

They spent the rest of the morning sharing little details of their lives. Doug gradually realized that she always managed to turn the conversation toward his family, his work, his activities. He wondered about this woman he loved so deeply as he shared his stories about the neighbours, his concern for his students, his love of music, his old friends in New Lancaster and the pranks they had played on each other. He gradually recognized a clear reluctance on her part to share the facets of her family's relationships, and surmised that old festering wounds still lay beneath the scars. In light of her recent trauma he decided not to mention his concern. She willingly gave him her love, and for now, he could ask for no more.

Reheating Mrs. Clark's pot pie, they made lunch together, watched the noon news and yawned through a game show.

Doug looked at his watch. "We've got a lot to do today, dear, and we'd better get started.".

She fingered the dressing gown. "I'll have to go up to Fiona's and get my clothes."

He gulped. "I forgot to tell you. They're out in the trunk of my car."

She raised her eyebrows.

He stroked his chin "Poor old Harry . . . . so we won't bother about a license. I wonder if anyone will notice our signatures in the register at St. Jude's . . . . Probably not . . . So we'll just go on as if it never happened. Sometimes I wonder how it all happened so quickly . . . Oh about your clothes, After I read the letter. I planned to take them to you when you gave Fiona an address. And when I found you I'd never let you go again."

She prayed a silent prayer of thanksgiving for being loved by such a man.

He brought the bags inside and piled them in Michael's old room while she rinsed the dishes As they were finishing their coffee, he called Angus McKelvie.

"Angus, it's Doug . . . Are you busy today? Margaret and I want to talk to you about us getting married . . . Yes, that's right." He grinned at her across the table. "I know I'm a lucky man . . . Yes. We want to get married as soon as possible . . . I can't believe you said that, Angus . . . All right. We'll see you in a while."

"What did he say?" she asked as he hung up the phone.

He grinned. "He said when a couple want to get married as soon as possible, there's usually a father with a shotgun behind them."

They dressed and drove over to St. Andrew's where Angus was waiting for them in his study. The beaming Scotsman listened attentively as they told him their plans. "I usually advise couples to have some counseling before they take their vows," he said."

Doug cleared his throat. "We're not kids, Angus. This is the second time around for both of us. We know what to do."

Angus raised his brows. "You're not too old to make mistakes."

Doug looked at Margaret. "Are we going to make mistakes?"

She smiled. "The biggest mistake I made was not telling you I loved you a month ago." She turned to Angus. "How soon can we be married? I have to let Mrs. MacPherson know so she can get the time off work."

He leaned back in his chair. "Three days. You'd better get the license today if you want to do it on Saturday. I have a meeting at one o'clock that will last an hour or so, but after that . . ."

They agreed that three o'clock on Saturday afternoon would be quite suitable, and Angus walked out to the door with them. He put his arm around them and wished them a good day.

"I forgot about the licence," Doug said as they went out to the car. "If we're going to keep this a secret, we'd better drive up to Englewood. If you and I walked into the registrar's office here, everyone in town would know by supper time that I'm marrying the most wonderful woman in the world."

She squeezed his hand. "And we'll need rings."

"I forgot about that too," Doug said. "My brain must be turning to mush." He headed toward Main Street and noticed Ed's truck in the parking lot at the bank on the corner. "I'd better stop and talk to Ed about Saturday." He pulled in behind the truck as Ed came out of the bank.

"Are you playing hooky today, Doug?" he called. Walking toward the car he noticed Margaret. "Hello there. How was the trip?"

"I'll never forget it," she said brightly.

Doug touched his friend's arm. "Margaret and I are going to be married on Saturday, Ed. Will you stand up with me?"

Ed's face broke into a broad grin. "That's great news. Sure, Doug. I'd be glad to get you to the church on time."

"It's going to be a very small wedding. Just us and Fiona and you, and Amy, of course. We aren't telling anyone until afterwards."

"Well we've got to have a little party to celebrate. Margaret's a pretty special lady and you can't keep her all to yourself. Why don't we go out to the club for dinner Saturday night and have some music. If I'm going to prop you up at the altar, then I deserve a dance with the bride." He leaned down to look in the window. "Isn't that right, Margaret?"

She raised her eyebrows. "I guess we do have to eat supper . . ."

"Okay, Ed," Doug said. "I'll call Maisie and make a reservation for dinner for . . ." He turned to Margaret. "Do you think Fiona will bring a friend?"

"She might."

"And maybe we should invite Angus and Gladys too. All right, Ed. I'll make a reservation for eight people for six o'clock Saturday night."

"What time's the wedding?"

"Three o'clock."

Ed slapped Doug on the shoulder. "I guess you can find something to do until six o'clock, can't you."

"Look, Ed. We want to keep this quiet so tell Amy not to say anything to anybody about it, eh?"

"Sure." He reached in the window to shake Margaret's hand. "I'm really happy for the two of you. Doug's the best guy in the world."

She looked up at him with shining eyes. "I know, Ed. I know."

Snow flakes drifted across the highway to Englewood. Glancing toward her feet, Doug said "We'd better buy you some boots today too. It looks like winter could be setting in early."

Margaret was sitting very close to him, her hand on his knee. "Do you get a lot of snow up here?"

"Yes. But the drifting is worse. Sometimes the snow banks get up to ten or twelve feet in places along the highway."

"My goodness! How do you ever manage to get anything done?"

"You and I don't have to manage this winter. We're going to Italy, remember? The Etruscans?"

She patted his knee again.

They remained silent for a while remembering that day on the lake when he had told her about going to visit the archaeological sites in Italy. He had also said that he loved her and she had wept in despair. Now her cup of happiness was overflowing and she leaned over to kiss his cheek. He reached down to place his warm hand over hers on his knee.

The clerk at the license bureau smiled as she produced the forms. Douglas James Parker and Margaret Elizabeth Darwin smiled as they produced the necessary identification and the fee. When the transaction was completed they drove to a shopping mall and entered a jewelry store. "I want to buy you a diamond too," Doug said looking around at the display cases.

Margaret shook her head. "I'd rather you didn't."

"Why not?"

She shook her head again. "Let's not discuss it here."

They selected plain cut gold bands and left them to be engraved while they found a quiet corner in the food court and bought sandwiches and tea.

Doug seemed uneasy as he took off his coat and sat down. "Why don't you want me to buy you an engagement ring, dear?"

She lowered her eyes. "I can think of several reasons."

"Tell me."

"Well, first of all, I have a diamond ring, a very nice one, so I certainly don't need another."

"But that was from John . . ."

She reached for his hand. "I know, darling, and there are some things we can't change. My memories of John are no threat to you, no more than your memories of Janet are a threat to me."

He nodded in silence.

"And another reason why I don't need an engagement ring as a token of your love is because I already know how much you love me."

He sighed. "All right. But what's another reason?"

"I don't know how to say this so I might just as well come out with it. I don't know very much about your, about your financial situation. I don't know how much money you earn, or what you have in the bank. Diamond rings cost a lot of money, Doug. Maybe when you bought Janet her ring it was only a few hundred dollars, which still was a lot of money back then. But now . . . My goodness, you could easily spend several thousand dollars, and I don't want you to throw your hard earned money away on something like a diamond ring."

His eyes searched hers, a hint of a smile on his lips. "So you're worried about me and my money. All right, I'll tell you right off I'm not rich. But the house is paid for, and the car, and the boat. I have some good investments, and an excellent pension plan. You won't have to worry about the wolf howling at the door, dear. We can afford a few luxuries, a honeymoon in Italy . . . And if I think it's going to be a tight squeeze, I can always go back to teaching in the fall semester next year."

"I don't want it to sound like I'm worried about money, dear, but I think I should contribute my share to the household expenses."

He shook his head vehemently. "Absolutely not. You keep your money for yourself. You'll need it for clothes and . . ."

She grinned deliciously. "I can't spend the interest on half a million dollars on clothing."

He choked on his tea. "What did you say?"

"It's true. I have over five hundred thousand dollars in a blue chip portfolio."

"Margaret!" He leaned back in his chair, his hands dangling at his side. "I never dreamed you were rich. I mean . . . You never acted like you had a lot of money . . ."

She chuckled. "I didn't know I did either until two days ago."

He blinked.

"When I first came to New Lancaster, I thought I should save my money for when I needed to go into a care facility. I remembered how much it cost to take care of John . . .'"

Doug reached across the table and held her hand.

"After he died, I still had most of the money from the sale of the house along with a few investments and a small pension too. John's life insurance policy was yet to be paid so I left my power of attorney with Bill Davidson, our accountant." She shrugged her shoulders. "I let him think I was going on a holiday to England too."

Doug noticed the "too" and tucked this piece of information in his mental file on Margaret's hidden past. He nodded his head.

"When I came out of Dr. Green's clinic with a new lease on life, one of the things I had to do was go to the bank and get some money. Those taxis in Toronto had taken almost all my cash. Bill Davidson's office is in the same building and I dropped in to see him. He was away and I talked to his son instead. That's when I learned that John had taken out another policy years ago and the interest had been compounding for the last twenty years. After John retired he used to spend a lot of time sorting through his desk and files. When I found the deed to the house in the trash one day, I started keeping a close eye on what he was getting rid of. He must have disposed of the policy before that. Fortunately, the accountant had a record of it."

She smiled at Doug. "I remember walking slowly out to the street in a daze. I even pinched myself thinking it might be a dream. But it isn't, darling. The insurance policies paid over four hundred and fifty thousand dollars after taxes . . . And then there's the other investments too."

Doug leaned on his chin and gazed across the table at her. "And I was wondering if I could scrape together enough money to buy you a little car to buzz around town!"

She reached for his hand again. "Thanks anyway."

"People are going to think I married you for your money, Margaret."

"People don't have to know. Look, Doug. Money isn't anything we're going to argue about but let me contribute something here. How about if I buy all the groceries and you can pay the other bills? And how about if I pay for the tickets for our honeymoon? And why don't we go to Nairobi to see Michael and Dorian on the way? I remember you telling me if you were rich you'd like to travel. Well, we are rich, darling, so let's enjoy ourselves."

"You never cease to amaze me. And thank you. Visiting Michael is a wonderful idea. I don't know why I never thought of going to Kenya."

She drank the rest of her tea. "Stick with me, honey. You ain't seen nuthin yet."

He laughed like a young man in love for the first time and took her back into the mall to buy some winter boots. As they rode the escalator to the second floor, she noticed a boy beside a pregnant woman descending on the other side. "Jeff!" she cried.

He looked down at her as they approached. "Dickie!"

"How are you?"

"Fine. I've asked Santa for a sailboat for Christmas," he said as he rode past. His mother frowned and shook her head in exasperation.

"That's wonderful," she said and called after him, "You can take me for a ride next summer."

A puzzled Doug took her arm as they stepped off the escalator. "Dickie?"

"Jeff was one of the campers at Deer Lake. I taught him how to sail a little boat like Tinkerbelle. He wanted to know what he could call me besides Mrs. Darwin because all the counselors had bird names, you know, funny pet names? I didn't know what to tell him, but you had called me Moby Dick so I suggested that. He said that I couldn't be a whale. I had to be a bird, so he called me Dickie."

Doug shook his head and they went into the shoe department to buy her boots. Finishing their shopping, they picked up their rings and drove home. She watched the snow blowing across the road into the empty desolate fields. After a while, Doug asked, "A penny for your thoughts?"

She turned to him and sighed. "I was just thinking about Jeff. He's such a wonderful little kid. He told me all about Jesus, and being saved. I learned so much from that boy's simple faith in God . . . And now he wants a sailboat for Christmas. Did you see his mother's face? They can't afford anything like that on a minister's salary, especially with other kids in the family too. I wonder if Ted's sold his boat yet. Maybe I could buy it from him and give it to Jeff. What do you think?"

"You don't have to ask my permission now"."

She frowned. "Now? What does that mean? Will I have to ask permission after we've been married for a while?"

He shifted in the seat. "Good night! I didn't mean it to sound like that!"

Margaret blinked at the sharp tone of his voice.

He glanced out the side window. "And I'm not going to ask you every time I want to play golf or go fishing either. Now then let's have a marriage where we feel free to still be our own persons."

Is he fearing for his single freedom? Her intuition recognized an issue brewing in their new relationship and for the first time she wondered at the wisdom of their impulsive decision to marry., until Peter Spencer became involved. It was true Doug had asked her to go to Italy, but he had never mentioned marriage. His declarations of love seemed genuine, but perhaps he never intended to marry again . . . Had her former refusals of intimacy coerced him into proposing marriage as the only way he could get her into bed? And now that he had taken her to wife was he only fulfilling an obligation to take her to the altar as well? Oh God! What have I done? Did he really want to marry me? Really and truly marry me? If I had gone to bed with him a month ago would he have married me then? Or would we have gone to Italy as just another foolish couple in a tawdry relationship? Oh God ! He never mentioned marriage until after . . . But he did say he wanted to take care of me though . . . But that's not the same thing is it ? . . . Oh God! . . . She shuddered at the thought that she had committed such a blunder in their relationship.

He sensed her sudden apprehension and touched her hand. "Are you all right, dear?"

She drew a deep breath and nodded slightly.

"I know we'll have to make some adjustments to the way we do things," he began. "We've got used to being on our own, haven't we . . . And I'll respect your decisions, Margaret . . . But it's a good idea if we talk about the things we want to do."

She drew another deep breath. "And that's exactly what I was doing, dear. I wanted to know what you thought about me buying the boat for Jeff."

He shrugged his shoulders. "Okay. I think you can't go around giving hand-outs to every poor little kid in the world. You'd be broke in a couple of weeks."

"But Jeff is special . . ."

"They all are."

She sat silently for several moments weighing the conflict. "I don't know, Doug . . . I feel like God wants me to do it."

He glanced at her before turning back to watch the road. "Are you sure it's God? Or is it you?"

She waited for a long minute and replied, "It's God."

He tipped his hat back on his head. "But how can you say that? How do you know? You've met a little boy and he tells you he wants something and because you don't want him to be disappointed, you naturally want to meet his need. So you bring God onto the scene to make your argument seem plausible. That doesn't seem right to me. You shouldn't use God to support your own motives."

She thought for another minute. "No. And I'm not doing that."

"It sure sounds like it. Jeff's probably a nice little kid but you can't say God wants you to do this or that when it's just your own natural instinct. Don't get yourself in a stew about this, Margaret."

She knew he had turned to look at her as she stared at the highway and wondered how to refute his argument. Twisting her fingers she said quietly, "Maybe it is my natural instinct . . . Maybe it isn't. And I'm not in a stew either. I just feel this is what God wants me to do."

"You feel . . . See, I knew you were getting emotional about this."

"All right, Doug . . . Let me rephrase that sentence. I know this is what God wants me to do."

Doug stepped on the brakes so suddenly and pulled the car over to the shoulder of the road. She wondered if he was angry.

He turned to face her. "I don't understand all this business of you and God talking together. Is this more of your POTSS?"

She bit her lip, struggling to make sense of his dilemma. Help me, God . . ."No. This isn't POTSS. It's the sanest thing in my life. My relationship to God is the anchor that holds me fast. It's the glue that keeps me together. If it wasn't for knowing Jesus Christ is always with me, I doubt I would have survived the accident to be here with you now."

He looked through the windshield at the blowing snow. "But when you talk about this God business, it's like I don't know you. It's like you're somebody else."

She watched his hands clutching the steering wheel.

She twisted in the seat to face him. "Look, Doug . . . The other night coming home on the train, I decided if you still loved me I would become your wife because I felt God had this planned for my life. He wanted me to commit myself to you, just as I've committed myself to Him. And now, for better or worse, I belong to you. You've become flesh of my flesh, bone of my bone. I don't need Angus to make me your wife except in the legal sense. I'm already your wife because God has made it so. You've filled every inch of my being with your love, just as God has filled me with Himself too. And I can't get away from either of you. I listen to you, Doug. I know what you say is true. But God is also with me, and He talks to me too. And sometimes it's like I hear His voice as clearly as I hear yours."

He stared at her helplessly. "I don't understand you, Margaret. I don't understand your God . . . All this talking back and forth . . . ."

She said softly, "Then just believe this for now, Doug. God loves you. He's just waiting for you to really discover His love and then you can truly love Him too. The understanding will come later."

He remained silent, trying to grasp her concept of God and form one of his own . . . Transport trucks lumbered by, rocking the car slightly as her words hung suspended in the frosty air. A sharp rap on the window roused them to see a police officer bending down to peer inside. A flashing light on the cruiser behind, shone through the gathering dusk.

Doug rolled down the window.

"May I see your driver's license and ownership papers please?"

"Sure." He pulled out his wallet and leaned over to fumble in the glove compartment. The officer waited patiently.

"Are you having a problem, Mr. Parker?" he asked, glancing up from the licence.

"No. We just stopped to talk."

"Oh." He leaned down again to look in at Margaret. "Are you Mrs. Parker?"

She smiled. "Yes. Almost."

He frowned. "Almost?"

"We're being married on Saturday."

He nodded. "You'd better find a safer place to talk then. We wouldn't want one of these trucks rear-ending you and you'd have to cancel the wedding."

"Okay," Doug said. "We'll move along."

"Good luck," the officer said as Doug rolled up the window before pulling out onto the highway.

The cruiser sped past them and they drove home in silence, Doug still wondering about Margaret's familiarity with God and Margaret praying for wisdom in sharing her relationship to God with the man to whom she had committed herself for the rest of her life.

After supper, they sat on the sofa watching the fire crackling and shooting sparks up the chimney. "I suppose we should call our children and let them know what we're up to," Doug said.

Margaret remained silent. He twisted his neck around to look at her. "What do you think?"

"I think I don't want to."

He frowned. "Are you ashamed of me or something?"

"Oh no," she said quickly. "But I'd hate it if Charles and Bruce and their families thought they should come rushing up here to the wedding. I'm not ready for them, Doug. Maybe it's my POTSS or something but I don't want to have all the fuss and bother of my family. We were emotionally away from each other for a long time and it's going to take a while to re-establish those family ties. I love them but I don't need them any more. Does that make sense to you?"

Unwilling to probe, he nodded. "I think I understand how you feel. Would you mind if I called Anne?"

"Of course not. She's your daughter . . . She's close to you."

"She may want to come home . . ."

"And she's welcome. I'm looking forward to meeting her."

He went out to find the portable telephone and dialed her number. "Hello Dick. Is Anne there?" He came back to sit down on the coffee table near Margaret. "Anne . . . It's me. I'm calling to let you know that Margaret has agreed to marry your old man . . ." He laughed. "Yes. I finally talked her into it . . . Sure . . . We've set the day for this Saturday. Can you make it home?" He raised his eyebrows. "Oh, okay. Well, we don't want to wait. We're not getting any younger, you know . . . Angus is going to tie the knot and Ed wants us to go to the club for dinner afterwards . . . Well I'm sorry you can't make it, dear . . . Margaret says she's looking forward to meeting you too . . . All right, we'll talk to you again . . . . Goodbye . . . I love you too."

He laid the phone down. "She can't make it. Too busy at work."

Margaret held out her hand to him. "So I get to keep you all to myself for a little longer."

Sitting on the coffee table he slumped and sighed.

"Is something wrong? Are you upset because she can't come to the wedding?"

He shook his head. "No. It's this business of her and Dick living together. She's my daughter and I want a man who's committed to her. I want her to have the security of a marriage, the emotional security. All these people who want to live together . . . It's like they're a bunch of kids playing house, and when the game is over they go and play house with someone else. It's not right, Margaret. I remember Angus quoting something about the marriage bed being undefiled . . ."

Margaret felt a burden lifting from her soul and she said softly, "That night, when you asked me to go to Italy with you, were you asking me to marry you?"

He gazed steadfastly into her eyes. "No."

She raised her eyebrows.

"You were so reluctant to let me get close to you, I knew you'd refuse an offer of marriage. But I hoped maybe you'd come as a friend. I didn't want to leave you behind."

Tears filled her eyes as she slid from the sofa to kneel before him. "What did I ever do to deserve a man like you, darling?"

The alarm clock rang at seven to another grey morning.

"So what are you going to do today?" Doug asked as he came into the kitchen where Margaret was buttering toast. "Will you need the car?"

She turned to straighten his tie and replied, "No. I'll tidy up around here and give Fiona a call later. I want to let her know about Saturday. By the way, have you called about the dinner reservation?"

"I forgot all about it." He rubbed his face. "Since you showed up, I haven't been able to concentrate on anything. I'll have to get my mind in gear for classes this morning."

She smiled. "You've been teaching history for so long, you could probably do it with your brain tied behind your back."

He laughed. "The upper classes are a challenge. Some of those kids like to argue, and I have to stay on my toes or they'd shoot me down in flames."

"You're going to miss them, Doug."

He stood up and put on his sports coat. "Nope. You'll keep me on my toes too."

She walked out into the garage to kiss him goodbye and returned to an empty house. After two days in his constant company, she felt a lonely happiness as she leaned on the counter and watched a weak morning sun attempting to break through the clouds across the lake. Cleaning off the breakfast table, she walked into the bedroom to make the bed when the telephone rang. She looked at it for a moment, wondering if she should answer it . . . It rang again and she picked it up and heard Doug's voice. "Hello, dear."

"Oh it's you . . ."

"Is anything wrong?"

"No. I didn't know if I should pick up the phone. If a neighbour or friend was calling you and heard me instead, they'd wonder, wouldn't they."

He laughed. "I'm just calling to say I miss you already."

She lay down on the bed. "I miss you too, darling. I really do."

He cleared his throat. "Well I'd better get going. I've got a lot of exam papers to mark today. I don't want my school work to interfere with my homework . . ."

She laughed. "I'll see you tonight, dear."

He hung up the receiver of the pay telephone in the hall and turned to see some male students watching him.

"Good morning, Mr. Parker," they chorused.

He smiled brightly at them. "It sure is."

His fellow teachers saw little of him that day because he spent all of his time in his classroom marking papers, shaking his head at the idiocy of some students, and drawing happy faces on the papers of others. When the bell rang later in the afternoon, he packed his briefcase and headed home.

"Margaret?" he called, entering the kitchen to the smell of cider warming on the stove.

She came quickly out of the bedroom. "I didn't hear the garage door," she said, kissing him.

"I left the car outside. Do you want to go some place? Do we need anything at the store?"

"I just need you," she said.

Afterwards, he looked around the bedroom and asked, "So what did you do today?"

She stretched. "I talked with Fiona. Saturday's fine for her and she's asking Mike if he'd like to come to dinner with us. You did call Maisie, didn't you?"

He rolled over. "Yes. It's all set. So what else did you do?"

"I unpacked my clothes . . . I hung them in the closet in the spare room. Some of them anyway. I'm getting rid of a lot. They're so old and out of style. Fiona wants to take me shopping tomorrow at Englewood."

"Oh?"

"And I made a list of some groceries we'll need. I can get them tomorrow too. And I made an appointment at Sally Dixon's to get my hair done on Saturday morning. Fiona's getting hers done too so we'll go together. She says I should sleep at her house on Friday night because you're not supposed to see me on our wedding day until the ceremony."

"Oh?"

"She said something about it being bad luck."

"You don't believe that, do you?"

"No. I don't believe in luck any more."

"I don't either. Besides, I couldn't sleep a wink if you weren't right here beside me. I missed you so much today. You said something yesterday about being flesh of my flesh, and bone of my bone. That's so true, isn't it. I sat at my desk and ached to be back here with you. Is this feeling ever going to go away? Am I always going to live on the edge? I never felt this way with Janet and I loved her too."

Margaret turned and looked at him for several moments. "I dunno. I'm trying to remember what it was like with John . . . Maybe it was this way at first. But we were younger and had a long future ahead of us and we were busy with things and people. You know, setting up a home, planning for a family. That's all behind us, Doug. We've been there and done that. All we have now is each other. And I'm happy with that, truly happy. There's a poem that I love . . . When we go to Toronto, I'll bring home some of my books so I can read poetry to you in front of the fire on a cold winter's night. That sounds romantic, doesn't it. But the poem goes something like this `Grow old along with me, the best is yet to be . . .'"

He stroked her cheek.

"Browning's wife, Elizabeth, also wrote poetry. They had eloped to Italy, and one enchanted afternoon she read her sonnet to him. `How do I love thee? Let me count the ways . . . I love thee with the breath, smiles, tears, of all my life! And if God choose, I shall but love thee better after death.'"

Sudden tears came to his eyes. "That's beautiful."

"I think so too."

"We'll take the book to Italy and you can read it to me some enchanted afternoon."

"All our afternoons are enchanted. Look. The sun is shining at last."

They went out to the living room and watched the sunlight on the muddy waves sweeping across the bay to crest near the pier and break onto the rocks. At the end of the lawn the drab willow leaves clung to the drooping swaying branches and dry brown maple leaves from the neighbour's yard swirled and danced toward the jetty. Near the house the pine trees hugged themselves and whispered to the wind.

They spent a quiet evening together, Doug at the desk marking papers, Margaret on the chaise thinking about the letter she was writing to her sons.

Doug took off his glasses and turned to watch her, the lamp shining on her light brown hair, her face now serious, her teeth chewing on the end of her pencil. He rose and went over to sit on the chaise at her knees. "You're looking very solemn, dear."

"It's my letter to the boys. I want it to be right. I want them to like you."

"Here, let me read it."

She handed him the pad and watched his face as he scanned the page.

Dear Bruce / Charles,

By the time you receive this letter I will have been married to a very wonderful man here in New Lancaster. I could write pages about Douglas Parker and who he is and what he does, but I won't do that, not now. Someday soon, you will meet him and will see for yourselves why I love him so very, very much.

Please don't worry that your mother in her declining years has flipped her lid or something like that. Believe me, I am anything but declining. I have a renewed zest for life that I would have never thought possible several months ago. I don't want you to think that my commitment to another man in some way detracts anything from my marriage to your father. We have all those wonderful memories of an honourable man who loved and cared for us so well. And I know he would be so proud of you both, as am I, to see you as caring husbands and fathers to your own families.

I will enclose the address and telephone number of our home here in New Lancaster. And it is a beautiful home, not just because of its situation and design, but because of the love we share together within its walls. I will call or write to you again when we have finalized our plans for travel early in the New Year. We haven't even thought about Christmas. Maybe we can get together then.

Be happy for me, my dears. Wish us well. We both send our greetings to Mavis and Jennie and the children.

Love always,
Mother.

He looked up and smiled at her.
"What do you think? Does it sound all right?"
He handed it back to her. "There's just one thing . . ."
She raised her eyebrows.
"Maybe you should change 'declining' to 'reclining'."
She laughed and swatted him with the paper pad.

During his coffee break on Friday morning, Doug called Angus McKelvie, "Angus, I was just thinking maybe we should have a few flowers tomorrow . . . Something to brighten up the front of the church. Could you could order a couple of baskets or sprays or whatever they call them . . . Yes . . . I don't want to do it myself because we aren't telling anybody we're getting married until afterwards. And while you're at it, would you order a nice corsage for Margaret? . . . I guess pink roses . . . Yes . . . And are you and Gladys free tomorrow night? We're going to have dinner at the golf club and we'd like you to join us . . . Thanks, Angus. Keep the bill for the flowers handy and I'll take care of it."

Jake McLeod, the principal of New Lancaster Secondary School walked into Doug's classroom during the lunch hour with a hint of a smile on his face. "So how's it going? Have we got any Rhodes' Scholars in this lot?"

Doug pushed the exam paper away. "I think we'd be stretching it if half of them graduate on the Honours List."

Jake walked over to look out the window. "I hear you're getting married."

Doug jumped up off his chair. "Who told you that?"

Jake turned around wearing a broad smile. "My wife's sister called her from Englewood last night and wanted to know if she knew a Douglas Parker in New Lancaster. It seems her husband, who's a cop, stopped to investigate a parked car and found a old couple in an amorous embrace on the side of the highway."

"What!"

"Doug, my boy, it's one thing to goof off, but getting picked up by the police is something else. What are the parents around here going to say when they learn a respected member of the faculty is making out in broad daylight on the side of the road?"

Speechless, Doug clenched his fists and wanted to punch Jake McLeod in the nose. He drew a deep breath. "It wasn't anything like that. We had just stopped to talk. That's all."

Jake nodded. "I know. I'm just kidding. I made most of that up. But my brother-in-law said the lady told him you were to be married. So who's the lady, and when's the big day?"

"Margaret Darwin, and Saturday." Still upset, Doug was trying to calm himself.

Jake raised his eyebrows. "Do you want some time off for a honeymoon?"

Doug unclenched his fists. "No. We're going to Italy after I retire . . . Kenya too, along the way. I want Michael to meet Margaret. She's a wonderful woman. We met last spring when she moved up here from Toronto."

"I think I saw her picture in the paper. She'd won a trip to the Bahamas."

"Yes."

"Pretty lady. Very attractive. Well, I won't keep you from your work. The last thing you'll be doing this weekend is marking exams." He patted Doug's shoulder and left the room.

Doug sat down at his desk and sighed. "This damned town," he muttered under his breath. "Margaret was right. You can't get away with anything." Forgive me, God. It's not a damned town. It's a wonderful place but I wish everyone would mind their own business!"

He went home after school to an empty house because Margaret was out shopping with Fiona. Still marking papers when headlights flashed in the driveway, he went outside and helped carry in bags of groceries. "I thought you two were buying clothes," he said as he staggered in with another armload of paper bags.

"We did that too," Fiona said. "Margaret's going to give you a fashion show tonight."

He leered convincingly. "I can hardly wait."

"Will you stay for supper, Fiona?" Margaret asked.

"No thanks. Mike's picking me up at six-thirty. We're going bowling. I'd better run. I'll see you at ten tomorrow morning, okay?"

She pulled the door shut and left them smiling at each other. "So how was your day?" Margaret asked as he held out his arms.

"Fine. I'm getting caught up." He had decided to say nothing of his conversation with Jake. "And how did you make out?"

"Fine. The stores are getting busy with Christmas shoppers already."

"And where are all these clothes you're supposed to model for me?"

She smiled. "That Fiona! You're not going to see some of the stuff until tomorrow night. She took me to a lingerie boutique and I never saw anything like it in my life!"

"I'll bet I haven't either."

"I did pick up a couple of sweaters and skirts though." She decided not to tell him that she had also bought a very expensive wool crepe dress, a soft creamy coloured creation that Fiona fell in love with when Margaret tried it on in the dressing room. A plain modest wedding had been a foregone conclusion from the outset of the discussions with Angus McKelvie but Margaret knew she had nothing in her closet suitable to wear in the stark sanctuary at St. Andrew's. The dress was now hanging in the closet of her old room at Fiona's. After their visit to Dixon's salon, they would return to dress for the ceremony and Fiona would take her to the church.

On Saturday morning, Doug retired to his desk determined to finish marking the examination papers. The clock in the hall had struck one before he stuffed the last one into his briefcase and went into the bathroom to shower and shave. He pulled another of Anne's gifts from the drawer, a white silk shirt, and tucked it into the slacks of his black suit, the suit he had bought to wear to Janet's funeral. The royal blue tie enhanced his eyes, and as he buttoned the silken wool fabric of the vest he thought it ironic that he should wear this same suit to the wedding with his second wife. "I'm opening another chapter of the book," he murmured as he turned off the light in the bedroom and walked out to get into the car and drive to the church.

Fiona's car was still in the driveway and he glanced at his watch. They still have plenty of time. I wonder what Fiona thinks about all this. And what will Margaret wear? Does she have a dress to drag out of her closet too? Some dress with memories from another life." Oh God . . . I'm so happy today. And I promise you, God, I'm going to take care of this woman you've given to me. I'd die for her if I had to. I know she's still got some problems from her past . . . Her sons . . . Please let them be kind to her." He smiled suddenly." Now she's got me talking to you, God. And that's okay, isn't it . . . And somehow, I even have this feeling that You're actually listening."

He pulled into the parking lot at St. Andrew's and noticed several cars. Wondering if Angus was still at his meeting, he went into the church and saw two huge baskets of white roses amid yellow, bronze and burgundy chrysanthemums flanking the altar. Satisfied, he walked through to Angus' study.

His pastor looked up and smiled. "Ready for the big day, Doug?"

"I guess so." Doug took off his topcoat and hung it on the hall tree.

Soon the front door of the church banged shut and he recognized Ed and Amy Haskett's voices as they came down the aisle. Angus rose and went out to speak to them. "Yes. The shorn lamb's waiting inside. He looks like he needs a friend."

Doug stood up and grinned. "I'm not that bad, am I?"

Amy came over to adjust his tie. She was looking slim and trim in her mink jacket and a dark green dress. "Don't you pay any attention to Ed. He's been making jokes all the way over here. I think he's turning out to be a dirty old man."

Doug smiled and glanced at Angus. He appeared not to be listening as he dug through the filing cabinet for the church register. "And where's the license, Doug?"

"Good heavens! I forgot it."

Ed burst into laughter. "See, Amy, I told you he was in Lalaland."

She shook her head at him. "Where did you leave it, Doug? Ed and I can run over to the house . . ."

"It's out in the car, in the glove compartment. The rings are there too."

"Well, give Ed the keys and he'll get them for you. If he's going to be your best man, he'd better start acting like one." She patted his hand and said, "Now all we need is the bride . . ."

Doug glanced at his watch. "She still has five minutes."

"I'm looking forward to meeting her. Ed says she's really nice, lots of fun."

He nodded. "She's wonderful, Amy. I know you'll like her."

They heard a blur of voices and Ed led a laughing Margaret and Fiona into the study. Margaret shook Angus' hand and turned to Doug. He introduced her to Amy Haskett and as the women made polite conversation, Doug watched his bride. She was wearing more make-up than usual and he thought it was Fiona's touch. Her green eyes seemed darker, her cheek bones, more prominent, her lips, fuller, her hair, more elaborately curled. As he reached to take her coat, he noticed her dress, beautifully cut, softly draped, a creamy colour that suddenly made the rest of her appearance exactly right.

Amy noticed it too. "My that's a beautiful dress. You look gorgeous in it."

"Thank you, Amy. Fiona took me shopping."

Fiona had opened the corsage box on the corner of the desk and came to pin the pink roses on her shoulder. "There," she said. "That's perfect." She turned to Doug. "You've got very good taste."

"I chose Margaret, didn't I?"

Fiona found a carnation in the box too, and pinned it on his lapel. "And she chose you too."

The organ began playing and Doug looked at Angus. The minister shrugged his shoulders. "I couldn't marry you without some music, Doug. Are we ready now?" Ed gave Fiona her ring and they assembled themselves in some degree of order with Mr. McKelvie leading them down the hall into the sanctuary. As Margaret and Doug stepped through the door they heard voices singing *"Praise my soul, the King of heaven."* The choir was standing about the organ smiling and singing exuberantly. Doug waved to them and tucked Margaret's hand closer under his arm.

"Dearly beloved, we have gathered here together . . ."

After the ceremony, the choristers sang another of their favourite hymns, *"Oh love that will not let me go"*. Amy Haskett, sitting in the front pew with Gladys McKelvie, wiped her eyes as the notes faded into the rafters, and Angus placed his hands upon the couple's heads. "The Lord bless thee and keep thee: The Lord make His face shine upon thee, and be gracious unto thee: The Lord lift up His countenance upon thee and give thee peace. Amen."

The choir descended to congratulate the newlyweds with hugs and kisses and then the wedding party went into the study to sign the documents as Fiona snapped pictures. When Mr. and Mrs. Parker were ready to face New Lancaster, Angus accompanied them to the front door and said he and Gladys would join them later at dinner.

Ed shook Doug's hand. "Well old man, Amy and I have to run along now and do some errands. We'll see you later." They went over to get into their car.

Fiona kissed Margaret and Doug again. "I know you're going to be very happy. I've got to pick Mike up soon so I'll see you at the club."

Doug took Margaret's arm. "The car's around in the parking lot."

"I feel kind of let down now after that wonderful music and all," she said. "I wonder what they think we'll do now."

He grinned. "I wonder . . ."

"Do you know what I'd like to do," she said suddenly.

"What?"

"See Jack Ferguson's car across the street? How about if we go over and tell him about us getting married?"

"Sure."

They walked over to the Baptist Church and she led him toward the pastor's office. Mr. Ferguson was sitting at his desk when Margaret called from the door, "Hello . . . Are you busy?"

He rose quickly and came out to the hall. "Margaret! And Doug! It's nice to see you." He noticed the corsage pinned to her coat and glanced at their hands. "Do my eyes deceive me or have you two just been married?"

They laughed happily. Doug said "Yes. We were on our way to the car in the parking lot at St. Andrew's and . . ."

"And I said 'Let's go tell Mr. Ferguson'."

He shook Doug's hand. "Congratulations." Turning to Margaret, he kissed her cheek. "And my very best wishes to you both."

An awkward silence ensued because none of them knew what else there was to say. Jack Ferguson squared his shoulders. "Would you like to come in for a while? That is unless you have some place you have to go."

"Not at the moment," Doug said. "We're having dinner at the golf club at six, but we don't have anything else to do until then."

They followed the pastor into the study and were seated in comfortable chairs. "So," Jack Ferguson said, crossing his legs. "How long have you been engaged?"

"About five days," Doug replied.

Jack burst into laughter. "Forgive me," he said trying to control himself. "I've heard of fast workers in my day but you take the cake, Doug."

"I've been chasing her for months," Doug said. "She finally caught me the other night."

"Doug!" Margaret shook her head at Jack Ferguson.

He smiled. "You're looking very well, Margaret. I've been praying for you . . . Uh, I guess you've told Doug . . ."

She suddenly realized what he was trying to say. "I've got so much to tell you, Mr. Ferguson," she said. "I scarcely know where to begin . . ."

He leaned over to pat her arm. "It's Jack. And it usually helps if you start at the beginning."

"Well, you remember when I was here to see you and we talked about putting my house in order . . ."

He nodded.

"Well, I have."

Doug leaned back in the chair and listened to his wife pour out her heart to Jack Ferguson. Some of it, he knew. Most of it, he didn't. He listened to her describe her spiritual battles with repentance and forgiving, lying and lust, and gained new insight into the dimensions of her relationship to her family. He learned more of her acquiescence to death and the beginnings of a remarkable journey to find God. He listened again to the description of her desolation on the island in the Bahamas and how the Lord had ministered to her in every way. Tears came to his eyes as he envisioned her in a hotel room desperately crying out to God, `I want to live!' He experienced her joy as the doctor had told her of the mistaken diagnosis. And he held out his hand when she reached for his and said, "And now I've come home to New Lancaster and the most wonderful man in the world."

Jack Ferguson had slumped down in his chair in awe of the adventures and mishaps of the woman who sat before him. He gazed at her for a long minute before he straightened up to say, "I don't believe I've ever heard anything like this in my life. You could write a book."

She shook her head. "No I couldn't. I've shared this with you because I know I can trust it to go no further. New Lancaster isn't ready for me. And Doug and I just want to blend into the scenery. We're looking forward to a quiet, blissful old age."

Jack Ferguson chuckled. "I should warn you, Margaret, that when you become a Christian there are no guarantees of blissful old age. You never know what the Lord has in store for you."

He turned his head. "And what do you make of all this, Doug? Can you be happy with a wife who has committed her life to Jesus Christ?"

Doug sat up straight in the chair. "Yes."

The pastor leaned toward him. "It may be difficult for you to understand her at times unless you're committed to Him too. There's something called divided loyalties."

Doug looked at him steadfastly. "I think I am committed, Jack. I love God. I think I've always loved God. Angus Mckelvie hasn't been preaching to me all these years without me understanding something. I know all about the fall of man, and the coming of a Saviour. Margaret seems to have a closer relationship with God than I do perhaps but . . ."

Jack Ferguson leaned toward him. "Several weeks ago I told Margaret that I sensed God was working in her life. I feel the same is true for you, Doug. I gave her a little book to read then and perhaps you will want to read it too. And if you do, you will learn about the need to make a definite choice to invite Jesus Christ to become your personal Saviour. That may be the difference between your relationship with Christ, and Margaret's. She can look back to a certain place and a certain time and say, "this is when my new life in Christ began . . ."

"My new life in Christ . . ." Doug repeated the words.

"Eternal life, Doug. Everlasting life. Read the little book and come back and talk to me again." He glanced at his watch. "Good heavens! Jean's going to kill me. We're supposed to be going out to dinner this evening."

Doug looked at his watch. "We must be on our way too. It's almost six o'clock."

Jack Ferguson walked outside with them and locked the door. "I don't want to steal sheep from Angus, but come back and visit another time. My door's always open."

He got into his car and drove away while they crossed the street to the parking lot. "This has been quite an afternoon," Doug said as he opened her car door. "I wish we'd invited Jack Ferguson to our party too."

The parking lot at the golf club was packed with cars and they had to park in the furthest corner. Hurrying to escape the cold wind, Margaret said "I'm glad you made a reservation. Is it always this crowded?"

"Not usually. Not unless there's a wedding reception or something."

"What do you think we're having, darling? Didn't we just get married?"

They were both laughing as they ran into the lobby and stopped to catch their breath. Ed and Amy came toward them and a band started to play "Here comes the bride". As a swarm of friends descended on them, they suddenly realized that the crowd was there for them and they burst into gales of laughter. Fiona came to take their coats, and Ed and Amy led them into the dining room, decorated with flowers and balloons and candles.

"I don't believe this," Doug repeated several times as Ed led them to a head table complete with a wedding cake.

"How on earth did you ever manage to do all this?" Margaret murmured.

"Organization, my dear. Organization. Amy and I love to have some fun. We just invited everyone to a party and they didn't know until they got here that it was a wedding reception for you."

"But it was such short notice . . ."

"When you live in a small town, it isn't that hard. The florist fixes the flowers, the baker does his thing, and Maisie gets extra help in for the kitchen. I even got Bobby Mills to come and sing for us."

She kissed Ed's and Amy's cheeks. "Thanks for being such special friends."

It was the beginning of a glorious evening. All the people Margaret knew had been invited, the volunteers with Meals on Wheels, the college students upstairs and their girl friends. When she saw Jack and Jean Ferguson slipping in the door, she nudged Doug and they laughed and waved to them. The toasts from the staff at the high school and the choir, the jokes about sailboats and trips to the Bahamas, and the abundant kindness of strangers made Margaret feel at home.

After the meal the band leader struck a chord and announced the bride and groom would have the first dance. Bobby Mills started to croon "Oh how we danced on the night we were wed . . ."

Doug took her hand and said, "Now we get to dance all by ourselves. It might be the last time tonight." He swung her out into a waltz and sang with Bobby . . . "Two hearts gently beating and murmuring low, My darling I love you so." Before she knew it, they had changed partners and she was dancing with Ed while Fiona was swinging around the floor with Doug. The rest of the night passed in a blur of laughter and music. At one point, she and Doug were walking among the tables thanking the guests for coming to the party and they came to the college students.

"Hey Ted. Have you still got Tinkerbelle?" Doug asked.

"Yeah. It's in the garage."

"Do you still want to sell it?"

Ted glanced at Margaret.

"No it's not for her," Doug laughed. "She's got a real boat now. We know a kid who wants a boat for Christmas. You name your price and we'll pick it up in a few weeks."

"Three hundred okay?" Ted asked.

"Sold," Doug said and stuck out his hand.

As they moved on to the next table, Margaret whispered in his ear, "I've never loved you more than right now."

He kissed her cheek. "Wait until you show me that fancy lingerie."

When Mr.McKelvie gave the announcements in church the next morning, he added, "I would like to thank Mr. and Mrs. Douglas Parker for the lovely flower arrangements they gave to St. Andrew's following their wedding yesterday afternoon." He lowered his spectacles to peer around the sanctuary. "I see they aren't here yet," he said in mock surprise. "I wonder what's keeping them." The congregation erupted in Presbyterian laughter.

Margaret Parker slipped quietly into the social circles of New Lancaster. She still delivered meals to her old friends and made a few new ones along her route. She and Doug were invited to several dinner parties as the guests of honour. The people of St.Andrew's took her to their bosom, and even Mrs. Clark had to admit that Doug Parker had found himself "a real nice missus".

She had called Dr. Green on Tuesday to get the results of the tests. "They're negative, Mrs. Darwin," he had said.

"I'm Mrs. Parker now," she replied. "I was married last Saturday."

Dr. Green chuckled. "I told you to get on with your life but you didn't have to do it so quickly."

She laughed. "I married a school teacher. Could we make the arrangement for any more tests the week after Christmas?"

"I don't see why that would be a problem. Give me your address and I'll send you a schedule of what Dr. Carson and I plan to do."

When Doug returned from school and learned of the conversation, he rubbed his chin and said, "He sounds awfully obliging. Do you think he's worried you might see a lawyer?"

"I'll set any fears at rest when I see him again,".

Charles and Bruce called as soon as they received their letters. Doug happened to answer the telephone each time and introduced himself to his new sons-in-law before Margaret spoke to them. They were happy for her, anxious to see them both, and each issued an invitation for Christmas.

Doug ran his fingers through his hair. "How are we going to handle this? When Anne hears we're in Toronto she'll want us too."

After some discussion they decided to remain in New Lancaster for Christmas and drive to Toronto on Boxing Day. They would stay at a hotel near the hospital rather than with any of their families. "We'll let them get used to us," she said. "And you'll need time to get used to them too."

Doug nodded. "It's just as well," he agreed. "I don't know what to do about Anne. Why couldn't she find someone her own age with no strings attached? I think I don't even like Dick."

"You sound like a father, dear. Maybe they haven't married because his divorce isn't final yet."

"I still don't like it," he grumbled.

"Christmas is coming. Be happy."

December arrived amid snow and ice, and as they spent a cosy evening in front of the fire, Doug asked "How'd you like to go to the Snowflake Prom?"

She chuckled. "I haven't been to a Prom for over forty years."

"If I retire, you won't be to another one for a while either. The student council makes quite a production of this and invites all the staff."

"Then we'd better not disappoint them."

The following snowy Friday night, the Parkers entered the winter wonderland of the school gymnasium. Silver streamers twisted among the giant white snowflake mobiles dangling from the ceiling. Hundreds of coloured lights on tall decorated pine trees in each corner blinked as the large room full of students romped to the disco beat. Doug led Margaret onto the floor. "I can't croon in your ear to this music, can I." She laughed as he shuffled his feet trying to find the rhythm. "I don't think I can even dance to it."

The disc jockey finally took pity on the faculty and played an old big band number. As Doug and Margaret swung about the floor amid the older couples, the students watched, some of the girls, wistfully, some of the boys, warily. One of the young men boldly came out onto the floor and tapped Doug on the shoulder. "I'm cutting in, Mr. Parker."

"Sure Gordon. Take her away." He turned to find a girl along the wall and danced with her instead.

Amused by the young man attempts to waltz, Margaret said, "I was hoping one of you fellows would ask me to dance. It's been a long time since I went to a high school prom."

Gordon awkwardly managed a turn and smiled. "I'm not a very good dancer when it comes to this kind of stuff."

"Relax," she said. "You're doing fine."

Several minutes later another young man cut in, and then another and another. The disc jockey kept the music playing continuously and after some time, Margaret wondered if there was any leather left on the toes of her shoes. The party was loosening up with the floor becoming more crowded as young people joined to dance the fox trots and two steps. Doug danced past Margaret with a variety of young ladies in his arms. The girls had started cutting in on each other too. "Hello, Mrs. Parker," he called.

She laughed with the young man she was dancing with. "Hello, dear."

They met at the punch bowl several times during the evening. "Having a good time?" he asked.

"Wonderful," she replied. "I'm not so sure my feet are though."

They went outside at the end of the prom to find a snowstorm sweeping in from the west. Cars slipped and slid in the parking lot full of fresh snow and when Doug's car got stuck, several young men came over to give him a push. By the time they reached Oak Terrace, the street was filling rapidly. "I'm not sure we'll make it home tonight in the car," he said. "This is when a four wheel drive would come in handy."

"Do you want to stop at Fiona's?"

"No. We'll try to make it."

They had to abandon the car less than a block from home. Wading through the drifts, Doug and Margaret finally struggled into the empty garage looking like two snowmen. Chilled to the bone, they shook off the snow and went into the house to soak in a warm bubble bath together.

The storm lasted through Saturday, piling snow against the patio doors. On Sunday afternoon when the snow ploughs came along Oak Terrace Doug used the snowblower to clean off the driveway and then walked up the street to claim his car with the engine packed solid with snow. The street lights had come on before he had shoveled his way out of the huge bank and two of the neighbours came to help him push the car into the garage to thaw.

Margaret met Doug at the door with a worried frown. She had never seen him look so pale and tired. He revived quickly but she went to bed that night concerned for his health.

After he left for school in the morning and Mrs. Clark was vacuuming the living room, she went into the bedroom and called Haskett's house. Amy answered and the women exchanged pleasantries about the storm and the season and Amy's grandson who was "growing like a weed."

Finally Margaret said, "By the way, is Ed around?"

"Yes. He's in the den. Would you like to speak to him?"

"Yes. Thanks, Amy." She heard a buzz on the line and Ed picked up the phone.

"Ed here,"

"It's Margaret, Ed. I want to ask you something."

"Sure. What is it?"

"The other night Doug and I were caught in that snowstorm on our way home from the high school prom. We had to ditch the car and walk the rest of the way. Yesterday Doug shoveled the car out of the drift so he could get it home to thaw out in the garage. He's not as young as he thinks he is and I don't want him doing this again so I've been thinking about buying him a four wheel drive."

"Whoa there, Margaret. That's gonna cost you a fair chunk of cash."

"I know Ed, but I can afford it. I don't want to tell Doug though because he'll say we don't need one. I thought I'd give it to him for Christmas with the excuse that I need a car to get around town, and this way he can have the new one and I can use his."

"You're looking at least thirty thousand, Margaret. Maybe thirty-five."

"That's okay. Doug's worth every penny and more. So I thought I'd ask you who I should go to. I've never bought a car in my life and I don't want some unscrupulous salesman taking advantage of me. Is there an honest car dealer in town?"

Ed laughed. "There is if he's talking to me. Look. Why don't I look into it for you and let you know how much and so forth. What colour would you like?"

She didn't even have to think about it. "Blue, to match his eyes."

"Okay. I'll tell Hank I want a four wheel drive to match Doug Parker's eyes."

She chuckled. "You wouldn't dare."

"Trust me, Margaret. And you aren't worried about paying for it? You don't need credit . . ."

"Absolutely not. Get me the best car for the best price and I'll write you a cheque."

"Did you win another lottery or somethin'?"

"No Ed. I had a very good first husband who provided for me, and now I want to take care of this one."

She made a second call to her accountant in Toronto. Bill Davidson, it seemed, had released his clients to his son. She made an appointment to see Jim between Christmas and New Year's, and asked him which investment she should cash in to buy herself a new car. He reviewed several options and she had no idea what he was saying. "All right, Jim. I'll leave it to you to look at the best tax break, and you can deposit fifty thousand dollars in my account here in New Lancaster."

There was a dead silence on the line. Finally, he said, "That's some car you're buying, Mrs. Darwin."

She laughed. "I forgot to tell you, Jim. I've married again. Now I'm a Parker. I suppose I'll have to change my name on all those papers, won't I. We'll do that when I see you in the office. And I'm not buying a luxury car. Just something to get me around town in all this snow!"

As Christmas drew closer, Margaret busied herself baking and shopping for the grandchildren. Doug had written to Michael telling him of his marriage and asking for permission to visit them early in February. Michael had written by return mail saying that he and Dorian were looking forward to their visit and little Julianne was already saying 'Gwampa' every time she saw his picture.

"I suppose it's too late to send something to her for Christmas, isn't it," he said after he read the letter to Margaret.

"Why don't we call them on Christmas Day. I'm sure there are all sorts of things they can't get in Kenya for her, and we could ask them to send us a list. She's still too young to know much about Christmas anyway so it shouldn't matter."

When Doug came home after the last day of school, he found a new wreath of evergreens and a silver bow hanging on the front door. Margaret led him into the living room where she had finished decorating a small pine tree. He took off his hat and sat down. "I haven't had a tree since Janet . . ."

"I found the box of decorations in the closet," she said.

"It sure is a dinky little tree. Couldn't we spend another buck or two and get a bigger one?"

"I was thinking of you when I ordered it," she smiled.

"Excuse me. Have I missed something here?"

"It's a living tree, dear. It's growing in a big pot of soil, and you'll have to carry it out of here before we go to Toronto. When Cook's delivered it, the fellow used a trolley. I was thinking perhaps we could wheel it out the sliding door on to the porch and plant it in the spring . . . After we come home from Italy."

He stood up to take off his coat. "I'm really looking forward to saying goodbye to all this snow. Italy can't come too soon."

Christmas Eve day dawned bright and clear . . . Margaret had located Jeff's address in the phone book and Doug had made arrangements to borrow Ed's truck to take the sailboat to Englewood that afternoon. Snow had drifted across Fiona's garage door and Margaret watched Doug grab a shovel from the back of the pick-up. When he had cleared the snow in front of one door, she found a spade inside and shoveled snow too. She had heard too many stories of healthy men like Doug dropping dead in snow banks.

Tying Tinkerbelle to the truck they set off anticipating a pleasant afternoon in the Christmas spirit. The streets of Englewood had even more snow than New Lancaster and they stopped several times to check the house numbers behind the mounded drifts along the street. "I think this is it," Margaret said at last.

Doug twisted himself around to back into the snow filled driveway. "You'd think Jeff's father could at least clean some of the snow out of here," he said. "If I get stuck again . . ."

"We'll call a tow truck," Margaret said. "I'll go in and make sure this is the right house."

She stepped out into a foot of snow and waded through foot prints to the front door. An empty,closed-in veranda ran the breadth of the wooden house. She rang the bell and heard nothing so she knocked sharply on the glass window in the storm door. The door to the house opened and an elderly woman shuffled across the cold porch to open the door. "Yes?"

"Is this the home of Reverend Davis? He has a son, Jeff?"

"Yes."

"May I speak to him or Mrs. Davis?"

"They're not home. Mrs. Davis is in the hospital. She's been sick."

"Oh my goodness," Margaret said. "I hope it's not too serious."

"It was. She lost the baby. They thought they were going to lose her too."

"Oh dear." Margaret bit her lip. "Is Jeff home?"

"No. He and the other kids are over at the neighbour's for the day. I've had my hands full ever since they got out of school. I'm not used to all the noise. I told the Reverend that I'd cook for them but those kids have wore me right out."

"My name is Margaret Parker, and my husband and I have a gift for Jeff. We'll leave it here in the porch for him if that's okay with you."

"Sure. It wouldn't be a sailboat, would it . . . That's all he talks about. How Jesus is going to give him a sailboat for Christmas."

"As a matter of fact it is," Margaret said.

The woman's jaw sagged. "You mean you actually have a sailboat for Jeff!"

Margaret nodded.

Her eyes filled with tears. "Well praise the Lord! Those poor kids. They're going to have a pretty lean Christmas with all the trouble they've had . . . Their father's just skin and bones trying to look after them all. The assistant minister is sick too so the Reverend's got the whole load himself. This sailboat is going to cheer them all up."

"Excuse me," Margaret said. "I forgot to ask your name."

"Judy."

"Did you have your appendix out this summer?"

"Yes. Why?"

"I took your place at Deer Lake Camp. That's where I met Jeff."

"Oh. Helen Stapleton told me you were a real help. I'm glad to meet you." She held out her hand.

Margaret shook it and said, "I'll get my husband . . . We'd better bring in the boat."

Doug had been patiently waiting in the truck, wondering about all the talking. When Margaret came back and told him the news, he shrugged his shoulders and said, "Let's get it unloaded before Jeff comes home and sees it. Maybe they can just put the paddle under the tree for him."

Judy tried to help them with the boat and they finally maneuvered it through the door and set it on the sun porch floor. "Isn't this grand," she said over and over again as Doug went back to the truck for the life belt and the sail. "Please come in and have a cup of tea. I've just made a fresh pot."

"Thank you," said Doug, rubbing his hands.

They sat down at the dining room table to sample some of Judy's cookies, fresh from the oven. "The Davises don't have a tree," Margaret murmured, glancing into the living room. "Don't they believe in having Christmas trees?"

"Oh yes," Judy said. "It's just been too busy for the Reverend to bother."

"The children are going to get gifts, aren't they?"

Judy shrugged. "Their mother may have bought something before she took sick. I haven't seen anything around here though."

As they drank their tea, they heard a rap at the door. Helen Stapleton bustled in leading several other women, their arms full of bundles and bags. "Well Margaret!" she cried. "What are you doing here?" She came over to hug her.

"My husband and I brought something for Jeff. I was sorry to hear about his mother and the baby."

"Yes. It was too bad. If there was a specialist in town it might have been different."

The other women were unpacking food and wrapped gifts. A man appeared in the doorway with a tree and Doug helped him bring it into the living room. Another man appeared carrying a roasting pan, heavy with a plump turkey.

"Mrs. Davis is coming home from the hospital tomorrow morning," Helen said. "We can't let Judy cope with everything so we've got all the fixings for Christmas dinner and enough food to last them for a week."

As Margaret and Doug drove out of the driveway, they met more of Mr. Davis' flock struggling through the snow bearing gifts for his family. She turned to him with tears in her eyes. "It restores your faith in humanity, doesn't it."

"It's Christmas. Peace on earth, goodwill to men."

The Hasketts weren't home when they dropped the truck off in Ed's driveway. "They're probably spending Christmas Eve with Brian and Midge," Doug said as he backed out to the street. "Do you miss your family on a night like this?"

"I don't know," she said. "I always feel nostalgic at Christmas time. I guess the child in me wants to go home. Do you feel like that too?"

He put his arm around her. "I'm going home and I'm a happy child."

As they approached the house he noticed a vehicle in the driveway. "We've got company. I wonder who it is." He pulled in beside a shiny metallic blue S U V and got out to look around for someone on his back doorstep. He came back to stand beside the vehicle shaking his head. "I wonder where they've gone."

Deciding to end the mystery, Margaret took a set of keys from her pocket and gave them to him. "Merry Christmas, darling."

"What!"

"Merry Christmas."

"Margaret! You're not kidding me, are you?"

"No." She grinned. "We've got stuck in our last snow bank. Open the door and let's have a look." She walked around to the other side and waited for him to release the door lock.

He sat in the driver's seat running his hand across the leather dash, looking at the panel of lights and dials. "I don't know what to say, dear, except thank you. I just can't believe you'd do such a thing."

"You do like it, don't you?"

"Like it? I love it! I'm going to be the envy of every guy in town. How much did you have to pay for it anyway?"

She laughed and poked him on the arm. "Don't even ask. If you knew, you wouldn't eat your Christmas dinner."

When they returned from the Christmas Eve carol service at St. Andrew's they walked across the back lawn toward the lake now silent under a blanket of ice and snow. "Don't you love the sound of your boots crunching in the snow," Margaret said. "And it's so beautiful here tonight."

Doug looked out across the white expanse. "Ah yes," he said. "And look at yonder moon. I believe it doth give the luster of mid-day to objects below."

She stopped to laugh at him. "You do know some poetry after all."

He chuckled. "I had to recite The Night before Christmas when I was in grade five and I still remember most of it." He shivered. "Let's go inside and nestle snug in our bed while visions of sugar plums and blue S U Vs dance in my head."

She was brushing her hair while sitting on the chaise when Doug came over to sit beside her. "I got you a little something, dear. It can't hold a candle to your gift to me but I want you to wear it with my love." He slipped an emerald ring on her finger beside her wedding band.

The large square cut gem flashed brilliantly in the lamp light. "It's beautiful, Doug."

He said, "It matches your eyes . . . See." He held her hand up to her cheek. "A perfect match."

She threw the hair brush on the bed and wrapped her arms around his neck. "We're a perfect match. Merry Christmas, darling."

Chapter Two

THE PARKERS LEFT EARLY TO drive to Toronto in spite of their fatigue from a previous busy day. Fiona had come for brunch because she was working the afternoon shift. Angus and Gladys McKelvie came for dinner. The Hasketts stopped by in the afternoon with Deirdre on their way to Midge's and Brian's for dinner. Ed was anxious to hear of Doug's reaction to the S U V. Deirdre was anxious to meet Margaret again and to see if she had changed anything in her late cousin's home. She was surprised and pleased to see it looked very much as she last remembered it. Watching Margaret, she thought if it were possible, Janet would approve of her and be relieved that Doug was happy at last.

Checking into a hotel near Thornbury Village, they made the phone calls to set up times for meeting their children, and then went down to the dining room for dinner. "It looks like a busy week coming up for you," said Doug as he scanned the menu.

Margaret nodded. "Yes. I'll be glad to get the doctor's visit over with tomorrow."

Dr. Green's receptionist smiled as Margaret introduced her husband amid the howls in the crowded waiting room. "It's good you're not waiting for the pediatrician this morning, Mrs. Parker," she said.

The clinic nurse, Mrs. Waters, raised her eyebrows as Doug followed Margaret down the hall into the examining room. If Dr. Green was surprised to see him there, he didn't show it and shook his hand, motioning him to a chair across the room.

"Any problems since you were here last, Mrs. Darwin, er Parker.?"

"No," she said.

"Any bleeding? Spotting?"

"No."

"Well, slip off your clothes and I'll come back to examine you."

"Margaret. I think I'll go out to the waiting room."

"I thought you wanted to stay . . ."

"I did. But I've changed my mind. Unless you want me to stay."

"Goodbye, dear. I won't be long."

Dr. Green examined her intensively, checking her lymph nodes, her breasts, her pelvis. "I think you're free," he said at last. "Dr. Carson wants another ultra sound on the ovary and a mammogram. The colonoscopy is set for Thursday morning. If that's clear we'll see you again in the summer . . ."

He helped her sit up. "Congratulations on your marriage."

"Thank you."

"Any problems physically?"

She smiled. "Nary a one."

"Any other problems, emotionally. You'd been under tremendous stress . . ."

"I'm much better. I think being terribly happy has been the best medicine."

He nodded.

She took a deep breath. "I don't want you to think I hold you in anyway responsible for what happened to me. Some people might take advantage of the situation but I assure you that I won't."

He nodded again. "Thank you. I appreciate your integrity. Will you tell that to Dr.Carson when you see him on Thursday. He's the one who's worried. But then he doesn't know you."

On their way to Charles' home after lunch, Margaret took Doug on a detour past Thornbury Village. Looking at the brick wall and the wrought iron gates, he said, "It looks like a prison.,"

"It was."

Charles and Mavis met them at the door with smiles and handshakes, hugs and kisses. They went into the family room and Margaret hugged her grandsons, taller than she remembered them eight months ago. Mavis' mother, Gertrude, brought in a tray of coffee mugs and greeted the guests warily. Margaret felt as though she was walking on eggs as she entered into a casual conversation about the Christmas activities. To relieve her tension, she inquired about the new addition to the house and Mavis conducted them on a tour to admire the results. Doug appeared to be at complete ease with everyone and often joined in conversation with the boys. Charles remained silent at times and Margaret knew he was microscopically examining his new step-father. She also felt Mavis' and Gertrude's scrutiny and wondered what Charles had told them about her deception and the reasons for it.

When Bruce and his family arrived before dinner, Margaret felt constrained to repeat her performance as the leading lady in the first act of the Darwin reunion. Fortunately, the children created diversions, and during a lull in the conversation, Jennie announced "I . . . Bruce and I are expecting a baby early next summer."

"There's nothing like a baby to bring people together," Margaret said on the way back to the hotel later in the evening. "I was beginning to wonder if I'd last through dinner."

"What do you mean?" Doug asked.

"Couldn't you feel it? Mavis? Gertrude? All those undercurrents of suspicion? They knew all about me lying to them last summer but they were too polite to say anything. I don't know what Charles told them. And Jennie too. They don't know how I felt or why I did it. And my sons. I think they understand, but the women . . ."

"Look dear. Don't worry about it."

"I know, but I feel I should say something to them, explain . . ."

He shrugged. "Wait and see what happens on Sunday when we go to Bruce's house. Tomorrow, I've got to deal with this Dick situation."

Saturday morning they drove downtown and parked in the garage of a luxury high-rise building. Anne opened the apartment door to welcome them in to her new home. "It's good to see you, Dad," she said . . . Margaret watched this blue-eyed, dark-haired, porcelain-skinned woman hugging and kissing her father.

"And this is Margaret," he said, turning to her.

"How do you do," Anne said.

Margaret leaned over to kiss her cheek. "I'm fine," she said with a smile.

A tall handsome man with broad shoulders and blond wavy hair came into the foyer. He held out his hand. "Doug . . ."

Doug held out his. "Dick . . ."

Margaret thought they looked like prize fighters squaring off for a match.

Anne said quickly. "And this is Margaret, Dick. Dad's new wife."

She shook his hand. "I'm pleased to meet you."

"Come in," he said pleasantly. "Lunch is almost ready."

They entered a living room with a wall of glass overlooking a park and sat down in a tastefully decorated room to talk about the weather, the trip from New Lancaster, the visit with Margaret's family and everything else that didn't matter to any of them. Dick rose and went into the kitchen.

"Is he cooking?" Doug asked quietly.

Anne nodded. "He's terrific. We're having salmon souffle for lunch."

Margaret chuckled softly and they turned to look at her. "I'm sorry," she said. "I shouldn't be laughing but I think this is quite wonderful. Where did you find a man who bakes souffles, Anne?"

"We met at work about a year ago," she replied. "Dick's a pediatrician and was up-dating himself in the neo-natal unit. I guess you could say I deliver them and he takes care of them."

The kitchen door swung open and Dick carried in a bottle of wine and a salad bowl. "Soup's on," he said. "Come and get it."

They moved to the dining area beside another wall of glass and feasted on a gourmet lunch, still making small talk. When Dick went out to the kitchen to bring in the cappuccino, Doug asked, "Have you been talking to your brother lately?"

"No," she replied.

"We called them on Christmas Day." He raised his eyes as Dick returned. "Dorian's expecting another baby."

"That's nice," she said. "How's she feeling?"

"Okay, I guess. Did I tell you Margaret and I are going to see them in February? We're making a detour on our way to Italy."

"Italy," Dick said. "I've always wanted to go to Italy. Is this a belated honeymoon?"

Doug nodded. "Yes. A nice long honeymoon after a very short courtship."

Margaret laughed. "And a very happy marriage, so far. I want to tell you, Anne, that I think you have a wonderful father. I'm sorry you and Dick weren't able to come to our wedding."

She and Doug related the details of the reception and the talk changed to their old friends of New Lancaster. Dick rose to clean off the table, and Margaret came to help him, waving Anne into the living room to sit with her father. As Dick loaded the dishwasher and Margaret started to wash the myriad of pots and pans in the sink, Dick came to stand beside her. "I don't think your husband likes me very much."

She turned to look up at him.

"I always get this feeling that he'd like to give me a kick where the sun don't shine."

She dried her hands and said, "Let's talk for a minute." She went over to sit at the breakfast table by another wall of glass and said, "Anne is the dearest person in the world to Doug."

"Except for you," he said. "I get the vibes between you."

She smiled. "He loves her and wants the best for her, that's all."

"And I'm not the best . . ."

"It's your living arrangements, your lack of commitment to Anne that troubles him. He wants her to have the security of a husband and family."

He sighed. "It's the M word, isn't it." He rubbed his face. "I was married once, and she left me to marry my best friend. That really hurt, Margaret. I thought I had the security of a wife and family, but I found out that I didn't. So what difference does marriage make? Oh I know I was at fault too. I was busy, too busy interning, too tired when I came home to be a good husband and father. But if she had just waited another year until I was finished, we could have made it. But I lost her and my kids and my friend."

He looked out the window and sighed again. "And then I met Anne. She's a lovely girl. And she's where I was, busy, busy with the pressure of her last year, and she comes home tired too. And sometimes I wonder if we'll make it. I'm here for her. I try anyway. But once you've been burned . . ." He looked away again.

Margaret reached out to touch his hand. "You love her, don't you."

He passed his hand across his eyes. "Yes."

"And she loves you?"

"She says she does."

"But does she really love you? You must be able to know that."

"I think so."

"What does she say when you talk about this, this insecurity."

He looked at her steadily, honestly. "We don't talk about it. I'm afraid to broach the subject . . . I don't want to lose her."

She shook her head. "Look Dick. I'm no marriage counselor but I've learned something about love along the way. I'm not talking about sex. I'm talking about love, the cement that binds two people together. And I've learned that if you want to win, you've got to be prepared to lose. I know that sounds silly but loving someone puts you in a vulnerable position. You don't base your love for someone on whether they love you back, the old what's in it for me game. You love someone for better or worse. You commit yourself to them completely, and when one partner feels this unconditional love, then it's easier for them to love you the same way. Perhaps your wife loved you and expected you to meet all her needs. I don't know and I can't judge her, but if she had loved you with an unconditional love then she wouldn't have been ready to turn to someone else to supply what you failed to give to her."

They sat together in a comfortable silence. At last he said, "I feel you have something more to say . . ."

She raised her eyebrows. "If I do, promise not to be offended."

He shrugged his shoulders. "Go ahead."

"Doug and I have found something wonderful together. And I owe it to the fact that we want God to be in the center of our marriage. And this raises our relationship above mediocrity to the sublime." She took his hand. "Look Dick. I like you. And Doug's not going to give you a kick in the pants either. But do yourself a favour and open yourself up to Anne, and to God. Give yourself a chance to become the man you ought to be. I'm sure you're a good doctor. I know you're a great cook and we'd better get this kitchen cleaned up before those two come in here to find out what's going on."

He smiled and went back to the dishes while she went back to the sink. They cleaned the place up and went into the living room where Anne was sitting on the sofa with her father. Margaret walked over to look out the window at the children skating on a pond in the park. "Would anyone like to go for a little walk?"

Doug looked up and she winked at him.

"That sounds like a good idea. Do you two want to come too?" he asked.

Anne opened her mouth to speak but Dick interjected, "Anne and I'll stay here and let you honeymooners be alone for a while." He walked them to the door and said, "While you're gone, I'll thaw out my apple streusel."

Doug shook his head. "If I hung around you for long, Dick, I'd be as fat as a pig."

He took Margaret's arm as they crossed the street into the park. "What are we doing out here? I wanted you to visit with Anne . . ."

"I can wait," she said. "I think Dick wants to talk to her now." She drew his arm close to her and told him of her conversation as they walked around the pond.

"I hope he's said what he wants to say," Doug said as they crossed the street again. "I'm freezing, aren't you? I think it's colder here than it is in New Lancaster." He rubbed his hands together. "Italy, here we come."

Anne met them at the door again with a big smile. "You both look like Rudolph," she said. "Dick's in the kitchen. If I hang around him much longer I'm going to be as fat as a pig too!"

Doug laughed.

"And I guess you can call me Miss Piggy because he's asked me to marry him."

Margaret's heart turned over as Doug caught Anne to his breast and kissed her. "And you said, `yes'."

She nodded with shining eyes.

He kissed her again and headed off into the kitchen calling "Dick! Aren't you supposed to ask the girl's old man for her hand?"

Anne looked at Margaret. "Thank you," she said.

Margaret put her arms around her daughter-in-law. "He's a good man. I know you'll be very happy."

They spent Sunday at Bruce's house. Charles and Mavis brought their boys for lunch, and as they squeezed around the dining room table, Bruce said, "We're planning an addition to the house as well as the family. We'll start in the spring."

After lunch, he took the boys outside to play street hockey, and Charles and Doug settled down in front of the television to watch a football game while the women cleaned up the kitchen.

Mavis asked, "Did you and Bruce plan on having another baby, Jennie?"

"No. Not exactly. We're quite happy about it though. The ultra sound shows it's probably a girl."

Margaret hugged her. "I'm happy too."

Jennie hesitated. "If it is a girl, Bruce wants to call her Janie. What do you think, Mom?"

Margaret sat down at the table with tears in her eyes. "I think it would be wonderful, Jennie."

"You wouldn't mind then."

"No. It would be nice to have a Janie in the family."

Mavis sat down across from her mother-in-law and folded her hands. "I want to say something to you, Mother. Charles told me about you going away last summer . . . How you thought you were dying, and you didn't want us around?"

Margaret said quickly, "I only wanted to spare you all the worry, all the care."

"But why did you have to make up the story about England?"

"Well, when I first told you that, it wasn't a story. It was true. I had really planned to go. It was afterward, when I learned about the cancer that I decided to go to New Lancaster instead."

Mavis twisted her rings and stared at the table. "When Charles came home and told me what happened, I started to feel guilty. You're my husband's mother and yet all I had been thinking about was my own mother instead. I had talked him in to providing a home for her, and never gave you a second thought. And after he told me about you thinking you were dying, I knew exactly why you wouldn't tell us. We had let you bear all the burden of John's and Jane's illnesses alone. God! We were awfully selfish to do that to you."

Jennie sat down at the table too. "Bruce and I thought the same thing, Mom. Bruce says you're all over this now but I want you to forgive me for how I treated you too."

Mavis was still twisting her rings. "And I want you to forgive me too."

Margaret took each of their hands. "Thank you for saying these things, my dears. I forgave all of you long ago when I was trying to get my house in order . . . When I was preparing myself to meet God. And now it's like we're all starting over again, me with a new husband, and you, Jennie with a new baby . . ."

They looked at Mavis and she quickly threw up her hands. "No you don't. Not me."

They broke into peals of laughter and Charles and Doug turned their heads toward the kitchen.

"So tell us about Doug and how you met and what you do in New Lancaster," Jennie said.

"Right now we've been shoveling a lot of snow," Margaret began. "No wonder Doug's looking forward to going to Italy."

"Yes. Tell us about Italy too," Mavis added.

Chapter Three

THE PARKERS DROVE TO NEW Lancaster a week later, looking forward to the peace and tranquility of their home. They had spent a busy ten days with their families, attending grandchildren's hockey games, visiting in their homes to play games and watch the boys devour all the food in sight. Most of Thursday was spent at the hospital in the radiology department and consulting with Dr. Carson who gave Margaret another examination before he was satisfied that she was free from cancer. They had an appointment New Year's Eve afternoon with Jim Davidson, reviewing Margaret's portfolio, revoking his power of attorney on her investments. "For your own protection," he had advised. "I'm not planning to leave town with anyone's money, yet though." She changed her name on documents and Doug asked for advice on his own investments as well.

They went back to their hotel too tired to celebrate the New Year. "Let's just have a quiet dinner and go to bed," Doug suggested. "All this visiting and the world of high finance is too much for an ol' country boy."

They lay down for an hour before dinner, woke up at nine o'clock in the evening and arrived downstairs in time for the New Year's Gala, a complete buffet and an orchestra. The `country boy' danced until the band went home at one o'clock.

Anne and Dick had come to a family dinner on New Year's Day at Mavis' and Charles' home and they blended into a friendly relationship that promised to continue on a casual basis. "It didn't hurt to have two doctor's on my side of the family," Doug said as he slowed the car to follow two logging trucks up a steep grade. "I think Charles is almost convinced that I'm not really a fortune hunter after all."

"Oh Doug!" Margaret protested. "He didn't think that at all . . . Did he? I mean he doesn't even know how much money I have. When I first suggested going to England he wondered if I could afford it. He is a bit of a stuffed shirt though, isn't he."

Doug smiled. "He's an accountant who likes all his ducks in a row. Maybe he should take up golf."

"Do you think all of them are going to come to New Lancaster next summer? Jennie and the baby?"

"We'll wait and see. The boys will love it, tearing all over town on their bikes. We can take them swimming and sailing. I'll make a sign and call it Moby Dick's Summer Camp for Kids. We'll be busy."

"We've got to get busy planning our trip too."

"And I've got final exams in three weeks too."

Bailey's Travel arranged their itinerary, and when Doug applied for a passport, Margaret asked Mr. Bailey to replace hers too. He looked at the stained pages in surprise. "Good heavens, Margaret. What did you do to it? Go swimming?"

She laughed. "Well you told me to watch my purse. And I didn't want to leave my passport lying around either."

They made piles of clothing on the beds in the spare room, wondering how much they could squeeze into their suitcases. One Saturday morning as Margaret was reviewing the luggage situation, the doorbell rang. "I'll get it," she called to Doug who was at his desk making up exams. She opened the door to find Jeff Davis and a tall thin man on her doorstep.

"Hi Dickie," Jeff said. "This is my father and we came to thank you for the sailboat."

She smiled and shook Mr. Davis' hand. "Please come in."

As they stepped inside, she called, "Doug! Can you come out here, please?"

She took their coats and led them into the living room. "This is my husband, Douglas Parker, Mr. Davis," she said as Doug came to join them.

The two men shook hands. "I'm Dan," Mr Davis said.

"And this is the sailor in your family," Doug said as he turned to Jeff.

Jeff grinned. "That's why we came to see you, Dickie. I wanted to thank you for the boat."

"We called it Tinkerbelle, but you can give it your own name," she said.

"No. I like Tinkerbelle . . ."

"Have a seat," Doug said. "And how's Mrs. Davis?"

"Yes," Margaret added. "I've been praying for her."

Dan Davis smiled and sat down. "She's much better. She's coming along fine."

"I think I'll make us a cup of coffee," Margaret said. "Would you like to come into the kitchen with me, Jeff, and tell me all your news?"

He sat on the stool by the counter as she busied herself with the coffee. "I want to tell you something, Dickie. Something God told me to tell you."

She raised her eyebrows.

"Remember when I saw you in the store . . ."

"Yes."

"And I said I asked Santa for a sailboat?"

"Yes."

"That was a lie. I don't even believe in Santa Claus."

"Oh?"

"You see, Dickie. I had really asked Jesus for the boat but I didn't want to say that in front of all those people and it was easier to say Santa instead."

"I understand, Jeff . . ."

"As soon as I said it I knew it wasn't right. And God told me I had to tell you about it too."

Margaret looked across her kitchen at his earnest face, loving this sweet child with his bright honesty. When she carried the tray into the living room, Doug stood up to move the papers on the coffee table.

"Guess what Dan has been telling me," he said.

She turned to their guest.

"His brother, Dave, lives in Uganda on the border with Kenya."

She cocked her head. "What does he do there?"

"He works at an orphanage. Most of the children's parents have died of AIDS. I'm sure there are other diseases too but 'the slim disease' has really devastated many families and the children are left to fend for themselves."

She sighed as she sat down and poured the coffee into the mugs. Jeff was sitting beside her munching on a cookie. "Someday, Dickie, I'm going to the Beyanatha and help Uncle Dave."

She patted his knee. "Maybe Mr. Parker and I will be able to meet your Uncle Dave, too."

Dan Davis crossed his legs and sat back in the comfortable chair by the fire and looked out the window across the dazzling snow-filled back yard under a brilliant blue sky. "The heat and the dust and flies of Africa will seem a long way from here, Mrs. Parker."

"Call me Margaret," she said.

Chapter Four

THE ENGINES ON THE 737 droned monotonously through the pale infinity above a brown wasteland. Margaret rested her head against Doug's shoulder, weary from the long flight across the Atlantic, and the clamour of the Fiumicino Airport before boarding Flight 4309 to Nairobi. Doug folded his newspaper and leaned over to look out the window. "Not much to see, is there."

She sighed. "How much longer?"

He looked at his watch. "Another hour. Have you changed your watch yet?"

"No. I'm too tired."

He smiled. "Here. Let me do it."

She held out her wrist languidly and he turned the hands forward seven hours. Resting his head against hers, he closed his eyes too, tired not only from the long journey but from the flurry of activities prior to their departure; his retirement parties, farewell dinners, family gatherings.

The Alitalia flight had left Toronto early in the evening, and set down in the bright sunshine of a Rome morning. As they entered the bustling cavernous terminal, Margaret yawned and looked at her watch. "It's almost three o'clock in the morning," she said. "Don't these people ever go to bed?"

They found their departure gate and collapsed in a corner of the lounge. Three hours later, they were winging their way up into the stratosphere for another long flight south, across half the continent of Africa. The sun was setting in a fiery blaze as the pilot announced they had now crossed the equator and would soon be landing in Nairobi's Jomo Kenyatta International Airport. Africa lay in shadows, a blur of dark shapes touched by scattered sprigs of lights. The plane banked to the left and suddenly, there beside them lay the treasure chest of East Africa, its jewels dazzling against the blue velvet night. The engine's pitch changed and the plane began the final approach into the airport south of the city. Awestruck by the beauty and symmetry of the modern glass terminal, Doug and Margaret walked along the circular corridor, looking for signs to baggage claims and customs.

"Dad!"

Doug turned quickly to see Michael striding through the crowd.

Margaret watched their reunion with a lump in her throat. She would have known Michael anywhere, brown curly hair, blue eyes, the proverbial chip off the old block. Doug turned to take her arm with tears in his eyes. "And this is Margaret."

Michael reached out to shake her hand. "We've been anxious to meet you."

She smiled brightly. "Is Dorian with you?"

"No. She's at home. We thought it might be too late for Juli. And Lulu couldn't stay tonight."

Doug cocked his head. "How did you get in here anyway? Aren't you supposed to wait for us on the other side of customs?"

Michael grinned, looking even more like his father, and showed them a blue plastic card. "I work for the UN. This card gets me into all sorts of places."

He picked up two pieces of their hand luggage and motioned them toward a moving walkway. They glided through a long glass tunnel suspended over parking lots and roadways to enter the main terminal. Bright lights glittered across ceramic mosaics on walls; small waterfalls splashed into green gardens, and colourful birds twittered in a corner aviary. Michael led them to the baggage claim, secured a porter to load the bags, and waved them through customs. A white Land Rover with the blue UN insignia stood close to the exit and within minutes, they had left Jomo Kenyatta and were heading northward into Nairobi along the Uhuru Highway.

Michael turned sideways in the driver's seat to include Margaret in their conversation. She had prodded Doug into the front seat and was now sitting in the back. "The Freedom Highway is part of a road system that runs from Capetown to Cairo," he explained. "Up ahead on our right is Nairobi Park. It's a wilderness in the suburbs. The wild animals range freely behind this chain link fence along the road. Once in a while someone complains about a leopard in their garden. Tourists find it intimidating that a lion can kill and eat a gazelle within a fifteen minute drive from the front door of the Hilton Hotel."

"Has a lion ever eaten a tourist fifteen minutes from the front door of the Hilton?" Doug asked.

Michael laughed. "Not lately, Dad. This whole country is like a big zoo. If you take certain precautions you're all right, usually. Once in a while you hear about something unpleasant happening though. A rogue elephant, a man-eating lion. There are some wonderful stories about the early settlers. When they were building the Lunatic Line . . ."

"The what?" Doug asked.

"The railroad," Michael explained. "Just before the turn of the century the British government was desperate to get a line of communication into Central Africa to forestall the German Colonial expansion. They decided to build a railway from Mombasa on the coast to Lake Victoria in the interior. It cost a huge amount of money and the parliamentary opposition called it `a lunatic line to nowhere'. The contractor imported over thirty thousand coolie labourers from India to work alongside the Africans. When they had moved inland several miles, a few old male lions acquired the taste for human flesh and feasted on the workforce, eating thirty Indians and many more Africans over a period of ten months. They were becoming so bold that one night a lion climbed on the train and took a European man who was sleeping beside his wife and children. The rascals were finally ambushed and shot."

The Land Rover passed the railway yards as Michael was speaking. Doug jerked his head toward the tracks and said, "I don't suppose you've lost anyone lately in there."

Michael laughed. "Don't worry, Dad. Canadians aren't on the menu. We're coming into the city now. This is recreational parkland and a golf course on your left and here are the parliament buildings on your right."

Doug and Margaret peered out to see floodlit gardens in front of an impressive sandstone building with Doric columns across its front facade. A huge statue stood near the street.

"That's Jomo Kenyatta, the first president of Kenya. He was in jail for almost seven years, convicted as a leader of the Mau Mau Rebellion. He was regarded as a hero by the tribes, and when Independence Day arrived, Jomo was there to guide the country through the chaos of assassinations, communist and capitalist maneuvers, and the pressures of all the independence struggles throughout Africa. The stability that the country enjoys today is due in large part to Kenyatta."

He swung the car to the right onto University Way. "Dorian works in that building to your left. Most of this property belongs to the University."

They looked blankly at a cluster of buildings behind huge trees.

"And now we're going to cross over the Nairobi River, what's left of it. In the rainy season, it's in full flood but now it's down to a trickle. We live up here in Ngara on Chambers Rd. I work at the UN complex about five miles further up this road."

He pulled into the driveway of a bungalow on a quiet street. "And here's where I call home."

Light shone through a large front window and an open door. A wide porch encompassed the house. As Michael began hauling out the luggage, a woman came to stand in the doorway. She disappeared for a moment and returned carrying a small girl wearing a cotton nightdress. Margaret walked up several stone steps and approached the porch. "Hello," she said. "I'm Margaret."

"And I'm Dorian." She opened the screened door. "This is Julianne She calls herself Duli. Michael calls her Juli so you can take your pick."

The little girl suddenly cried out, "Gwampa!" And wriggling out of her mother's arms she ran down the steps to Doug.

He set the bags down and caught her up in his arms. "How's my little baby doll?"

Dorian smiled at Margaret. "It seems she has another name now too." She came down the steps to greet Doug and help Michael with the luggage. "You two must be exhausted."

As Margaret entered the house, she noticed it shone. The tile floors in the foyer gleamed. The parquet floor in the living room glistened. The wooden furniture glowed. The glass table tops sparkled. Dorian led Margaret to a sitting room with a screened wall across the rear of the house. Beyond was another wide porch. She opened a door into a bedroom and stood to one side as Michael and Doug put all the luggage in the corner. Here, was a screened wall, and a shining glass door opened on to the porch too.

Dorian nodded toward a gleaming bathroom across the room. "Why don't you freshen up and I'll make a pot of tea."

Michael said, "Come with me, Dad. You can use our loo and let Margaret have a moment for herself."

Doug followed Michael back toward the front of the house and Dorian took Julianne into the kitchen across the sitting room. Margaret found them all there at the table several minutes later. Michael patted a chair beside his. "Sit down, Margaret. Make yourself at home."

Julianne was sitting contentedly on Doug's knee and Dorian was putting out some crackers and fruit on a plate. The kettle whistled and soon the family was seated together talking about the trip. Margaret sipped her tea feeling a numbness in her extremities and she knew she must lie down before she tumbled off the chair. She swallowed another mouthful and said, "I know you'll understand if I say goodnight. I really need to get some sleep."

Dorian rose. "Of course," she said, leading Margaret toward the bedroom. "I'm working in the morning but I'll be home for lunch." She folded back the striped bedspreads on the twin beds. "If you should need anything, Lulu will be here with Julianne and Mwangi will fix your breakfast when you're ready."

Margaret stripped off her clothing as the bedroom door closed and she crawled between the cool sheets, desperately dropping her tired head onto the soft pillow. She awoke in the middle of the night, reaching for Doug, realizing he was in the bed next to hers, the sound of his breathing comforting her in the stillness of the soft dark night. Somewhere outside, a lid of a garbage can clattered to the ground. She raised her head, listening. The fragrance of jasmine wafted through the screen. She lay in the silence, considering the circumstances in which she now found herself, the attractive, affluent home with evidence of excellent taste in decoration and the latest electrical conveniences. Michael and his darling daughter were exactly as she had imagined. But Dorian . . . Doug had not prepared her for Dorian. The gentle woman with a subdued sophistication wore her stunning beauty as a garment, casually, effortlessly. Her smooth mahogany skin, her dark eyes needed no external applications to add to her appearance. Her arched eyebrows bespoke some care, and her full lips under the straight nose were coloured only slightly. Her jet black hair pulled into a sleek coil and her straight posture added to her height. Margaret could easily understand how Michael had been smitten, and she wondered for a moment that their marriage had brought such disconcertion to their families. But as she lay and thought about it for a while, she realized that perhaps

Dorian had changed from the shy and defensive college student who had visited the bastions of an all-white small town in Ontario. She and Michael had moved into that global society where mixed-marriages were quite normal. He had made his life in a multi-racial business complex, and Dorian had come home to her roots, accepted for her skills in contributing to a burgeoning global community.

A wild fiendish cry pierced the darkness with another crash of metal. Margaret jumped and sat up in bed clutching the sheet. She peered through the screen, feeling an ominous presence near. Silence blanketed the neighbourhood again and she lay down wondering if she would ever go back to sleep. Doug turned over in bed. She threw back her covers and crept in beside him. Still asleep, he tucked her close. Secure now, she felt herself drifting into peace.

They awakened to the sounds of a reel lawnmower clicking across the lawn below the back porch. Doug squinted at his watch.

"What time is it?" Margaret asked groggily.

"Eight o'clock."

They drowsed in the comfortable warmth and woke again at nine to the sounds of shears clipping and snipping outside their window. "I'm so tired I can hardly move," Doug said.

"How late did you stay up last night?" she asked.

"We talked until almost eleven, I guess."

"No wonder you're tired. Did you hear some animal out here last night?"

"It was probably a hyena. Michael said they'd been having trouble with them scavenging the garbage. Dorian's coming home for lunch but Michael says he's tied up all day with meetings. He's taking next week off to show us the sights."

She stretched. "You see if you can go back to sleep for a while, dear. I'm going to have a shower."

He was sleeping soundly by the time she emerged from the bathroom. Quietly unlocking a bag, she found a change of clothing and dressed slowly, wondering how to address the servants who were somewhere on the other side of the door.

She found Mwangi in the kitchen chopping vegetables on the counter. A large pot sat on the stove. "Good morning," she said.

He turned to face her, his shiny dark face wreathed in a smile, his black curly hair cropped closely to his round head, his wide nose flattened above his thick lips. He wore an immaculate white jacket over a pair of faded blue jeans, a pair of loose sandals on his large pink soled feet.

"Habari ya asubuhi," he replied.

"Oh," she said. "Do you speak English?"

"Kidogo tu . . . A little."

"My name is Margaret Parker."

"Bibi Parker . . . My mistress."

A tall black matronly woman joined them. "Bibi Parker," she said. "My name is Lulu. Mwangi does not speak the English much."

Margaret smiled at Mwangi. "And I don't speak Swahili at all."

"Would you like some breakfasts?"

"That would be nice. Some coffee and toast would be fine."

Lulu turned to Mwangi. "Kahawa . . . Siagi mkate." She turned to Margaret and asked "Bwana ? . . . Mr. Parker. He will join you?"

"Later. He's still sleeping. Where is Julianne, Lulu?"

"She plays with her toys. Come out to sit on the porch and Mwangi will serve you."

Margaret sat at a round table on the wide porch at the back of the house and looked around the manicured garden. Roses bloomed in a sunny corner of the yard. Geraniums at least five feet high grew in profusion along the fence. A mass of delphiniums occupied another corner along with oleanders and hibiscus. The pungent fragrance of eucalyptus permeated the quiet morning air. Lulu returned with Julianne and an armload of toys. The little girl regarded Margaret from a distance.

"Hello Duli," she said.

The litle girl hid behind Lulu's ample girth. When she peeked around the full colourful skirt, Margaret said, "Boo."

The girl laughed and hid her face again. By the time Mwangi carried a tray of fruit, and buttered bread, and coffee out to the porch, Margaret was chasing Duli around Lulu and all of them were laughing together.

Doug stepped through the screen door of the bedroom rubbing his eyes. "Gwampa!" Julianne cried and ran along the porch to greet him. He picked her up and carried her back to the table where Margaret introduced him to Mwangi and Lulu. Mwangi retired to the kitchen to fix more breakfast for the Bwana, and Lulu attempted to remove Julianne from the scene too.

"No, no" Doug protested. "Let her stay with us. She's all right."

They sat on the porch the rest of the morning, drinking coffee, playing with Julianne and enjoying the warm sunshine while Mwangi cooked in the kitchen and Lulu ironed in the nursery.

Dorian returned home at noon, looking very elegant in a pair of cream coloured slacks with a long multi coloured cotton overblouse. She joined them on the porch and after several minutes, Doug decided he should shower and shave and get dressed for the day.

Margaret watched him disappear into their room and turned to Dorian. "So what do you do at the university?"

"I teach the undergraduates micro-biology," she replied. "They learn the basics of course, but now, there is an added emphasis on research into the mutating strains of viruses that seem to be such a plague in Africa. We are about to receive a huge grant from the UN to upgrade our laboratories with the newest micron 'scopes and all the computer-imaging toys. I may be going to the Disease Control Center in Atlanta for training on this equipment in the spring. That will be a real challenge for me and it's a problem with my pregnancy. And Doug says that Anne is planning to be married in early summer." She rubbed her cheeks. "I don't know what to do. It's such a long journey, isn't it. I know exactly how you were feeling last night, Margaret. And I don't want to put the baby at risk."

Margaret shrugged. "I've been thinking that we should have stayed overnight in Rome. It would have been less tiring for us. Would it be possible for you to do something of that sort?"

Dorian smiled. "I suppose so. I don't want to leave Julianne behind either, and she'd be a handful to travel with."

"How long would you be in Atlanta? And would Michael be able to leave his job then too?"

Dorian shrugged. "I don't know that either. He's got some holidays coming but I'm not sure he'd be happy baby-sitting in Atlanta for a month or so while I go to school."

"Perhaps he could take a week or two and fly to New Lancaster with Julianne. Doug would love that . . . And then you could come up too when you've finished your course."

Dorian stared grimly across the garden. "I don't think New Lancaster is ready for Michael and me, let alone Julianne And I won't have her hurt."

Margaret bit her lip. "Look, Dorian. You've been around enough to know that prejudice or intolerance isn't just limited to blacks and whites. It's everywhere, and there are probably billions of people who if they can't discriminate against someone else because of the colour of their skin, then it's their religion, or their economic status, or their ethnic origins or even their sex. What was the feminist movement all about? I can understand your concerns for Julianne. Believe me, I truly can. But on the other hand, I want to tell you that New Lancaster is an oasis in the world of injustice. I know this town and many of the people. They may have their personal hang-ups, but it's a wonderful place, and your little girl will never ever feel anything but love and acceptance among the huge circle of our friends and neighbours."

Dorian glanced toward the bedroom door and said quietly, "As long as I live I'll never forget the look on Michael's parent's faces when he introduced me to them for the first time. I thought I'd die . . ."

Margaret leaned forward and said "And Michael should have told them you were . . . black, or brown, or whatever you wanted to be called. And he should also have told them you were beautiful. I don't want to seem harsh but if he had prepared them before you met them, I'm sure they would have would have handled the situation differently."

Dorian nodded. "I know. I told my parents about Michael being white and they weren't too happy about him either at first. I wondered about Michael after I met his parents. I wondered if he was afraid of them, afraid to tell them, and then I wondered if he was ashamed of me! God! We had an awful fight that night. We walked along the beach in the dark and I raved at him, accusing him of all sorts of things, hiding in the anonymity of a city with his black girl friend, afraid to face his old friends with the ugliness of our relationship, afraid to confess to me that ours was a backstreet affair. I never realized that within my mouth lay the power to reduce this healthy, strong, vital man to a quivering, blubbering wretch. Michael changed that night. I guess I did too because we realized in spite of everything that had happened, that we loved each other and nothing would ever separate us again."

Margaret reached out to take her hand. "You know something, Dorian? I think I did the same thing with Doug. Someday when we have the time, I'll tell you about it too. I scarcely know your husband but he reminds me so much of his father, and if he gives you the same happiness that Doug has brought to me, then you're a fortunate woman. We both are, aren't we . . ."

Mwangi appeared on the porch and spoke rapidly to Dorian. She answered him more slowly in Swahili and he returned to the kitchen. "It's time for lunch," Dorian said. "I wonder if Doug will be much longer."

Margaret pushed herself out of the chair. "I'll go and tell him the soup's on."

Dorian laughed. "How did you know we were having soup for lunch?"

"You can call it a lucky guess. I'll never be able to learn the language."

They ate leisurely as the sun grew hotter directly overhead. By the time Mwangi served the custard dessert and tea, Margaret was yawning. "My goodness," she said. "I think I'm ready for an afternoon nap."

"It's the altitude as well as jet lag," Dorian explained. "It may take you a couple of days to get used to having less oxygen in the air. Would you like to lie down with Julianne ? She has a nap about now and Lulu usually has a siesta with her."

Julianne was happily surprised to see her new "Gwama" lying on the spare bed near her crib. Anticipating more fun and games she was disappointed to see her grandmother close her eyes and fall into a sound sleep. There was nothing left for her to do but curl up beside her rag dolly and go to sleep too.

Two hours later Margaret roused to Julianne jumping about in her crib. Lulu entered the room quietly to carry the little girl away. "It's all right, Lulu. I should get up now too."

Lulu smiled. "I take her for a walk now, Memsahab. Bwana Parker, he go for a walk already."

Margaret went out to find Dorian working at her desk in the corner of the screened sitting room. "I heard Lulu tell you that Doug has gone for a walk. I think the man didn't know what to do with himself."

Margaret smiled. "I think I should unpack a couple of our suitcases. We tried to separate our lighter clothing from the heavier things we'll need in Italy."

"You'll need some warm clothing here in Kenya too. It can get quite chilly in the evening, and if you and Doug should decide to drive up into the higher elevations it gets downright cold. Michael is planning to take a holiday next week and drive you down to the Maasai Mara Game Reserve. It's quite a spectacle."

"Will you be able to come too, Dorian?"

She shook her head. "I'll take the Friday off and we'll spend the weekend at Mombasa. It's lovely down there at the shore."

Margaret decided to unpack most of their things and was just setting the gifts they had brought on the bed when she heard Doug and Michael at the front of the house. She and Dorian went to greet them.

Michael smiled at Margaret and said, "You'll have to keep an eye on this man. There I was, driving up the hill and I see this fellow talking to a very attractive woman and I thought he looked an awful lot like my father. And he was!"

"Don't believe him, dear. The woman wasn't all that pretty, but her flowers were gorgeous. I've never seen gladiola like that before. Each blossom was as big as my fist. So I had to stop and admire them."

Dorian laughed. "That would be Mrs. Montgomery. She wins first prize at the flower show every year. Why don't we sit out here on the porch and I'll get us a tray of sundowners."

The Parkers soon realized why the observance of the Kenyan sunset became an aesthetic ritual for all but the most callous of Africans and tourists. A low wave of darkness broke far down the eastern drift of the plateau and as it swept on toward the city, the western sky became crimson as if the whole of heaven were inundated with fresh blood. The shining orb, now visible to the human eye through wispy veils of burnt orange and bright yellow sank lower into the flood and then dropped suddenly like a stone beneath the horizon. The colour faded rapidly as the golden dying rays reached up to grasp the last tendrils of a pale green sky and then it was dusk and the soft darkness covered the land.

Julianne appeared in Lulu's arms, bathed, fed, and dressed for bed. Doug took her on his knee as Lulu turned to Dorian and said, "I go now if you are okay."

Dorian smiled. "We'll see you in the morning."

After Lulu walked back toward the kitchen, Margaret asked, "Does she have far to go?"

"A little over a mile up the road," Michael replied. "Mwangi lives further still but he rides a bicycle."

Dorian rose. "I should go and see how he's coming along with dinner. He's been working on it all day."

Mwangi's culinary efforts were well rewarded by the compliments from the guests and hosts. He had roasted pieces of chicken in a spicy sauce, and served them on a bed of seasoned rice, surrounded by stir-fried chunks of plantain, pineapple, sweet potatoes and manioc. Small disks of unleavened bread were eaten topped with a spoonful of chutney. All of it tasted delicious but Margaret was at a loss to recognize any of the herbs or seasonings. After Mwangi served a sweet cake dessert drenched in a rich coconut sauce, he spoke to Dorian. She replied and dismissed him for the evening.

Michael shook his head and turned to his father. "Isn't she amazing. She picked up the language as easily as she picks up after Julianne."

Julianne was sitting in her highchair, chewing on a piece of bread and playing with a little toy from her grandparents' suitcase.

Doug turned to Dorian. "You do use English when you teach, I suppose."

"Oh yes," she replied. "When I'm working with the students in the laboratory, sometimes we switch back and forth, but all the technical terms are English. As we move toward the twenty-first century I'm sure the language will change as have many of the tribal customs. Actually Swahili is a relatively new language and I think it is still evolving."

Doug cocked his head to one side. "These tribal customs you mention . . . It's a good thing that they're changing. Some of the ones I read about seemed pretty barbaric . . . Female circumcision for instance."

Michael nodded. "Those customs, female circumcision, and male circumcision too, haven't changed as much as we might wish. I think what Dorian's referring to is the change in the tribal way of life. So many of these native people have been driven off their lands by their own government. In the pursuit of the almighty tourist dollar, the government has created all these national parks and game preserves . . . The Maasai Mara is a good example that we will see first hand next week. The noble Maasai warrior/ herdsman cannot live in most of his ancestral homeland unless he is a park employee of the Kenyan government. Thousands and thousands of acres of grazing land have been taken from these people, leaving them impoverished."

Doug moved Julianne to his other knee. "But that seems awfully unfair."

Michael shrugged. "What do you think we Canadians have done to our own native people?"

Doug nodded. "And it's gone too far now to turn it all around. There's got to be an answer to the mess we've gotten ourselves into but no matter what we do, there will always be someone who's unhappy with the solution."

Dorian stood up. "I'll take Julianne now, Doug. It's time for her bedtime story."

He yawned. "And I think I'm going to bed too. I didn't have an afternoon nap like someone else I know." He smiled at Margaret.

Margaret said "Well I'll clean up the table then."

"Oh no," Dorian said quickly. "Just leave it the way it is. Mwangi would be upset if we did his work. He'll be here as soon as it's daylight."

"He sure puts in a long day," Doug said. "I wonder what his wife thinks about him being away from home like this."

Michael laughed. "His wives, Dad."

"Wives? How many does he have?"

"I think it's three, isn't it, Dorian? He's considered a man of considerable status in his circle. We pay him well for his services. He knows it too, and this permits him to house three wives and their children in separate rondavels."

"What's a rondavel?" Margaret asked.

"It's a round, windowless hut with a conical thatched roof to keep it cool inside. I think they look like toadstools."

"Why don't we take them to the Bomas tomorrow, Michael?" Dorian asked. "We could have lunch somewhere and spend the afternoon in town."

Doug stood up. "You can take me anywhere you want tomorrow, but right now, I'm taking myself to bed. Are you ready for bed now, dear?"

Margaret shook her head. "Not yet. I'd be awake at three o'clock in the morning. Perhaps I can read Julianne her story?"

She sat in the rocking chair in the nursery and looked at picture books until the little girl grew drowsy. Tucking her into bed, she went out to the living room where Dorian and Michael were watching the news on television. She sat for a while listening to the woes of the sub-Sahara, the effects of the drought, and the political fortunes of Nelson Mandela. Yawning several times, she decided it was time to go to bed and excused herself.

She undressed in the dark and closed the bathroom door quietly to brush her teeth. As she crept between the two beds, groping to turn down the spread, a hand grasped her knee. She jumped and stifled a squeal.

"What are you doing?" he whispered.

"Trying to go to bed."

"Well get in this one instead."

"You're supposed to be sleeping," she whispered as she slipped in beside him. "You said you were tired."

He put his arms around her. "Not too tired."

Dorian drove her bright blue Fiat around the market square and found a parking space outside the Muslim's Women's Hall. An enterprising young man wearing a long white kanzu approached the car. His thin brown face bore traces of Arab ancestry and his diction seemed quite different from Mwangi's. Michael gave him several coins and turned to his father. "I was just feeding the parking meter. These chaps stake out a piece of the street. If you pay them well, they will guard your car with their life. If you don't, your hubcaps could disappear or even your car. This chap knows us and so far we haven't had an incident."

They jostled their way through the crowds of Saturday morning shoppers in aisles of garden produce, fresh killed meat covered in flies. Shouting women's voices filled the air as they haggled for cloth, clothing, food and jewelry. Margaret chose a woven kikapu to carry on her arm while Dorian negotiated the price with the vendor. She and Doug bought the traditional safari hats and laughed as they looked at their reflections in the small warped mirror on the wall of the stall. "Just call me Frank Buck, big game hunter," Doug drawled.

The deceptively powerful sun at noon on the equator bleached the sky of colour, leaving an intense white light. The Parker family decided they had had enough of the market, retrieved their car still intact, and drove two blocks to Kenyatta Avenue and the heart of Nairobi's business district. They turned east onto the broad tree-lined boulevard with ample parking spaces on either side of the four traffic lanes. Michael turned to Doug and Margaret in the back seat. "Nairobi gets its name from an old Maasai word meaning cool water. When they were building the railroad through here, the contractor decided all this flat land would make a good depot so this is where he settled in. The land was bald, bare as a bone, not a tree in sight. As the railway brought settlers with the promise of cheap land, a local government was established and the first administrator set about to bring some shade to Nairobi's dusty tracks. He knew nothing about Kenya's indigenous trees and didn't bother to learn which trees grew quickly or hugely. Instead, he opted for the tried and true, and imported all sorts of trees from Australia and America. As you look down Kenyatta Avenue, you can see what I mean. Over there are the fast growing blue gums and grevilleas from Australia. In October the huge jacarandas burst into bloom with a lilac and mauve haze. The bougainvillea bloom year round, and you can see the many different kinds of palms . . ."

"Michael. Sorry to interrupt but where are we going for lunch?"

"Let's try for the Thorn Tree."

Dorian slowed the car in front of a large sidewalk cafe in front of the New Stanley Hotel. "It looks pretty crowded, don't you think?"

"Okay," he said. "We'll try the Norfolk instead."

Dorian found a parking place near the long veranda overlooking the dry Nairobi River and Doug thought he was stepping back in time to Elizabethan England. Black beams and white stucco lent a mediaeval air to the old hotel and he wondered what ghosts roamed the premises at midnight. Fans whirred overhead as they sank into comfortable rattan chairs on the shady porch. "The hamburgers are pretty good here," Michael said. "The local beer is quite good too but it's twice as strong as the imports."

"Then I'll steer clear of that stuff," Doug said. "Unless you want to leave me here to nap all afternoon."

Michael glanced at his father. "You're feeling okay, aren't you. All this isn't too much for you, is it?"

"For Pete's sake, Michael! I'm not over the hill yet. Margaret, tell him I'm still in the ball game."

She laughed. "I've never seen you play ball in your life, Doug, so what do I know. Don't worry about him, Michael. Your Dad's doing fine."

They ordered hamburgers and a pitcher of iced tea and sat back to enjoy the ambience of the Norfolk Hotel's veranda. "This is a nice place," Doug observed, glancing around. "It looks quite new."

Dorian sat up and poured another glass of tea. "It is and it isn't. Most of it had to be rebuilt several years ago after a bomb exploded here at a New Year's Eve party. There were many casualties . . ."

Margaret looked out over the shady gardens. "It seems so peaceful here. Why a bomb?"

"Who knows?" Michael replied. "After the Israeli raid on Entebbe in Uganda to rescue the hostages, there were all kinds of anarchists and terrorists seeking revenge." He turned to his father. "The Norfolk was first built at the turn of the century when Nairobi was probably like a town on the American frontier. It's had its share of cowboys and Indians too. There was one character who's become a legend . . ."

"Like Davy Crockett?"

"More like a cross between Paul Bunyan and Billy the Kid." Michael leaned back in his chair and crossed his legs. "After they built 'the lunatic line' the British government was desperate to recover their investment so they opened the country up to white settlers, completely disregarding the fact that several tribes already lived here. The Brits encouraged these settlers to develop plantations for sisal, coffee and tea mostly, and the land produced good crops. The whites hired the Africans to work for a pittance and there were incidents of unrest but nothing much really happened. Many of these settlers were the rootless middle sons of the minor British aristocracy. They had some access to the family fortunes and received the financial assistance to begin their African adventure.

"One fellow, a Lord Delamere from Cheshire, settled on a hundred thousand acre ranch in the Rift Valley. The Maasai people didn't know what to make of this little, cranky red-haired man. Lord Delamere has since been nick-named the Red Baron. He had seen the Maasai herdsmen grazing their cattle and decided to import some very expensive Australian sheep. He grazed them on land the Maasai would never think of using. It was mineral deficient and all the sheep died.

"Then he ploughed the land, planted English clover, restocked with more sheep, and watched the clover fail because the African bees couldn't pollinate it. Undaunted, he imported English bees. They were quite successful in this regard, but because there was no winter to give the crop a dormant period, and no frost to kill off the pests, the clover grew into a huge green jungle and all the sheep died of foot rot."

Doug and the women began to laugh at Michael's narrative. He continued. "And so the Red Baron gave up sheep farming and turned to cattle, cross breeding the beef stock from Cheshire with the hump-backed, long-horned cattle of northern Kenya, rightly thinking that these would be resistant to the local viruses. But there was a new bug that came up the coast from German East Africa, and he was wiped our again!

"By now, the Maasai took pity on this 'mad' Englishman. They took over what was left of his herd and cross-bred with their own animals, grazing them on the land they knew could support them. Delamere became a great friend of the Maasai, and now that his ranching venture was on track, he turned to agriculture and once more showed his fellow settlers how to go bankrupt growing sisal and hemp. And he brought oxen in from South Africa to plough a vast acreage and planted wheat. At last he had something that would grow, but unfortunately, the news spread by way of the jungle express, and every wild animal in the Rift Valley came for breakfast, dinner and supper. And what they didn't eat was destroyed by several species of wheat rust! He spent another fortune to develop a rust-resistant strain, and solved the problem with the animals by shooting everything in sight. And that got him into trouble with the civil servants in Nairobi."

Michael's audience was shaking with laughter.

"Yes, the Red Baron was quite a fellow. After months of isolation in the Rift Valley, he and his cronies would ride into town here for some fun. He'd lead the charge down the street out there shooting out the glass oil lamps, steeplechasing through garden parties and other genteel soirees. Sometimes they'd lock the chief constable up in his own jail. The Red Baron always stayed here in this hotel and after a night of heavy drinking, his friends would play shuttle board with his inebriated body on the long counter in the bar. One memorable evening they had a horse race through the lobby, jumping over the chairs and furniture. When the manager protested, they threw him out into the street. Nairobi was always relieved when the Baron returned home to the Valley." "So what finally happened to him?" Margaret asked.

"He became a champion for the rights of dispossessed Africans, especially his Maasai friends. A very young Winston Churchill came here on a safari and after the Baron took him on a pig-sticking party, W C changed his African policy and, as Churchill's political fortunes waxed and waned, so did the tribal rights. And of course after a drunken dissolute adventuresome life, death claimed the Baron."

"And here, endeth the lesson," Dorian said, brushing the crumbs from the tablecloth. "Are we ready to head out again for more African culture?"

They circled the business district to drive past the city landmark, a twenty-seven story round building with a large amphitheater in the shape of a rondavel beside it. "This is the Kenyatta Conference Center," Michael said.

Doug and Margaret looked out across a huge parking lot to the magnificent building. Bougainvillea and other flaming vines added to the riotous landscape of colourful shrubs and flower gardens. Dorian swung out into the left lane of the Uhuru Highway heading south. "Are you going to remember to drive on the left hand side of the road?" Margaret asked Doug.

"I sure hope so," he grinned.

"That's becoming an issue too," Dorian remarked. "Wherever the British settled in Africa, the population drives on the left . . . But most of Africa is now right hand drive, and the car imports are designed for that too. One of these days we're going to have to change."

"That could be chaotic."

Michael turned around to smile at his father. "Driving in Kenya is already. Here in Nairobi we seem to be fairly orderly, but get out into the country and it's every man for himself. Some of these drivers invented the word `kamikaze'. I can't blame it all on the drivers though. A few years ago they added a tax to the price of gasoline to do road repair. The minister of transportation apparently transferred the funds to his Swiss bank account and left the country. So it doesn't really matter what side of the road we're supposed to drive on. The top priority is to avoid the potholes or risk wrecking your car."

They passed the rail yards and entered the wide open spaces of the Nairobi Game Park. A few animals were grazing in the distance, indistinguishable in the bright intensity of the early afternoon sunshine that shimmered on the plain. They drove by the airport and finally turned into a large complex. Parking the car amid the tour buses,

Dorian took two large parasols from the trunk. "We're going to need these," she said, handing one to Margaret.

They walked toward the entrance as Doug fished in his pocket for the fee. "I'll get it," Michael offered.

"No. I have to get used to this money," Doug replied. He pulled out a bill with a 20. "You call this one a pound too, don't you?" Michael nodded. "Yes. That's a 20 Kenya Shilling Note. A KShs 5 is almost equal to a US dollar. You'll need another one of those KShs 20's to get us through the gate." The Bomas of Kenya was crowded with tourists that Saturday afternoon. Many of them were Japanese with cameras slung around their necks. Doug hung his camera around his neck too. "When in Rome . . ." he said.

They walked through a series of village settings where women pounded manioc roots, ground maize, stirred the cereal cooking in pots over fire pits. Some women sat on the ground feeding or playing with their children while others made string from piles of fibers and wove fishing nets, or strung colourful beads for necklaces and bracelets. Almost all of the women appeared to have shaved heads and were dressed modestly in loose dresses or wrap around sarongs. Some of them had donned elaborate multi-layered ropes of beads about their necks and arms, but most wore a simple braided headband and long looped ear-rings.

There were a few men in the village, sharpening spears, shaping bee hives from hollow logs, and one fellow sat at a potter's wheel fashioning a lump of clay. Several men were involved laying new thatch on an old rondavel as others twisted the straw into small bundles, tying it with another piece of straw. When the Parkers reached an amphitheater, they soon realized where all the men of the villages had gone. Decked in their most elegant finery, the young and old alike were performing for the wilting audience.

The Maasai warriors, taller than an average man, dyed their long thin braids with ocher dust. Red aprons covered their naked bodies and their long muscular legs were painted with intricate tracings. They carried spears and shields, and wore collars of beads and bright ear rings. Several Maasai stood out from the rest. These leaders had not dyed their hair and wore immense headdresses of lion manes and ostrich feathers instead.

The shorter Kikuyu men also wore elaborate headdresses of feathers, and bright armbands and necklaces of beads and feathers. Their short grass skirts swayed to the beat of the long drums their musicians hung from their necks and straddled with their legs.

The northern Samburu tribe paled in comparison to the rest, wearing a few strands of beads around their neck and torso and a short sarong. They carried long thin spears. Their only true adorning was a heavy dusting of ocher powder over their short hair and faces.

Other tribes were represented by smaller groups of men. One warrior from the western plains stole the show. His headdress of hippo teeth, antelope horns and ostrich feathers was at least four feet wide. He also wore a huge cowrie shell necklace under a sweeping fur cloak bedecked with beads and feathers as well. The flute player from the Giriama faded into the background with only several small feathers in his hair and a few bracelets of blue and white beads.

The Parkers sat in the shade of their parasols and watched the shuffling of bare feet in the dust to the incessant beating of the drums. As Doug took several pictures of the performance, he wondered about the primal traditions that had passed from one generation to the other. And sitting there in the heat of a Nairobi afternoon, Douglas Parker confronted his own soul. Watching these men shaking their beads and feathers, he wondered why. What's the point of it all? What's the significance of the feathers and the paint? Why the chant and the dance rituals, all this leaping about with the spears? Don't they have anything better to do with their time?

He closed his eyes against the glare of the sun and imagined himself back in time listening to the same chants to the same drums; a warrior of the tribe; his primitive urges only the age-old truths of survival and acceptance. A man could not live unto himself and survive in the world. He needed his brother to protect him, to affirm him as a man, to give him that essential ingredient of his humanity, communication, fellowship and even love. These rituals were ingrained into the fabric of his tribal existence as surely as the seasons with the life-giving rain. Traditions of honour and taboos took precedence in every facet of life. Women and cattle were to be possessed, used to further the power and wealth and position of the tribe. If a woman died in childbirth or of disease or overwork, it became essential to find another woman to work, to provide, to procreate, insuring the existence of the tribe. If cattle died of disease or were stolen then it was a man's duty to find more cattle, even to steal cattle from another tribe to maintain the family status.

Doug shuddered as he turned his thoughts inward to himself. In a way, I'm no different from these fellows. I have the same goals in my life, survival and acceptance. `No man is an island'. I need my tribe too, the camaraderie of my friends in the community and the workplace. But I'm different from these fellows too. Their traditions and values are not mine. My woman is not my possession. She is not my means to wealth, position and power. And yet, Margaret has brought me wealth in so many ways. Apart from the actual money, I'm a richer man because of what she gives to me, her care, her nurture, her provision. And she's given me a position too. Now I'm no longer `the extra man', `the odd man' seated at the table at Amy's dinner parties. I'm a husband again, and in a sense, the father to a much larger tribe. Has she given me power? Yes. Because I'm learning about her belief in God, Now I'm a much stronger man than I was a year ago. So am I different from these fellows after all? Margaret is not my possession. But in a way she is. Yes. She's my wife. We took vows before God to keep ourselves each to the other. I'll never let her go. But if she wanted to leave me, could I, would I make her stay?

And what about my responsibilities to my tribe, my country? I suppose if it were a matter of life and death, I would still go off to war. If my enemy was at the gate, I would defend my home . . . But who is my enemy? Or what is my enemy? I don't think I have to worry about the neighbouring tribe charging across the Canadian/USA border to rob me of my goods. But a nation can be diminished in other ways as well. We Canadians are losing our national identity. Has it been stolen from us, or have we lost it by apathy, or ignorance or greed? And what sacrifices am I willing to make to preserve the health and wealth of my tribe? Anything I might do would be lost in the enormity of the situation. Perhaps these fellows had a simpler solution. They didn't have to take on the whole world . . . Just the fellows over the next hill. Victory or defeat, winner take all. No compromises, no negotiations. Just lop off everyone's head, take the women and the cattle and head for home.

He felt Margaret poking his arm. "Are you sleeping?" she asked.

He shook his head. "I don't think so."

"Well, wake up and look at this."

He focused his eyes on the center of the ring where several Maasai had gathered about a long-horned cow, and one of the young men was squatted on the ground milking the teats into a long cylindrical clay pot. As he rose to his feet another Maasai with an elaborate lion's mane headdress approached the circle and stuck a sharp pointed knife into the neck of the animal.

The crowd gasped.

A spurt of blood traced through the air and the warrior clamped his mouth over the wound, drinking the blood. When he had his fill, the milker caught the spurting blood into the clay pot. Another man wadded together a handful of straw and mud and clapped it into the wound to staunch the flow while the rest of the men drank the mixture of blood and milk. The drums throbbed again, and as the cow was led from the ring, the warriors leaped high into the air in a dazzling display of strength and ferocity. They left the arena to the applause of the spectators.

Margaret shook her head. "Do they do this every day?" she asked Michael.

"Yes. It's the only opportunity a tourist has to see the old Kenya, and these fellows make a percentage of the gate so they do all right too. Are we ready to go home now?"

"I have to stop at the store for some milk," Dorian said. "Is there anything else we need?"

"Don't look at me," Doug said. "I stopped thinking about what was in the pantry the day Margaret married me."

Margaret chuckled. "So that's why you married me!"

He put his arm around her waist as they walked out to the car. Michael held out his hand to Dorian. "Looking at these two makes me feel like an old married man."

She laughed at him. "You'd better get back in the ball game, dear."

On the way home, she pulled into a side street in front of a large food store and left the motor running as she dashed inside. Michael turned to point to the sign outside `Gutra M Singh, Prop.'. "The East Indians have just about taken over the country," he remarked. "They're very enterprising in their pursuits and control most of the retail trade now. It's a little odd because the Africans hold the political power but the Indians have the financial clout, and of course money talks the loudest in the end."

Dorian returned carrying two glass bottles of milk. "I hope these will be all right, she said. "The clerk told me the refrigerator's been off most of the day and they're still waiting for the repairman. I took the tops off and sniffed, and they seem okay."

Michael sniffed the milk too. "We shouldn't leave it too long, dear. In this climate, we can't be too careful."

They spent Sunday, resting in the shade of the veranda, reading books about the Serengeti-Mara experience, dozing off in the middle of the page, and waking to the queries of an active little girl who wanted someone to play with her. Lulu had Sundays off, Dorian had said. Lulu spent most of the day in church.

"We should have gone to church," Margaret said to Doug.

"Are you a Presbyterian too?" Michael asked.

She glanced at Doug and smiled. "I guess so. I used to be an Anglican, but your Dad's settled in St Andrew's so I go there too. You can throw a little Baptist my way for flavour though. I guess I make myself at home whatever church I happen to be in."

Doug sat up in his chair, awake now. "How hard is it to get into Uganda?"

"Not very. Why?"

"We know a fellow back home whose brother works at an orphanage near Jinja. A place called Beyanatha or something like that."

"An orphanage, eh?" He turned to Dorian. "That's probably the place that takes in all the AIDS victims."

"That's it," Doug said. "That's the one. I have half a notion to drop over there and say hello to him from his family."

Michael nodded. "I'll get you two used to touring around Kenya before I set you loose in Uganda. It's a pretty wild world out there, Dad. We don't want you getting into trouble."

They left Dorian and Julianne on the front veranda very early Monday morning and headed across town to Ngong Road and the rolling green hills leading toward the southwestern edge of the plateau. The early rains had brought a welcome reprieve to the drought stricken escarpment and as Michael's Land Rover bounced its way toward the edge of the Rift Valley, Margaret and Doug gazed out upon the empty undulating veldt. Rounding a shoulder of the road they suddenly found themselves in a grey void. Out-croppings of volcanic rock pierced the barren soil and the only visible vegetation was a solitary thorn tree, its sharp spines warding off any beast in search of nourishment.

Michael stopped the jeep at the crest of a rise. "Let's get out and stretch our legs. We still have a long way to go."

They stepped out into the bright sunlight and cool fresh air of early morning. Below, the world dropped into a gaping chasm. Their senses reeled as they grasped the immensity of the blue African sky stretching across the void to distant lavender hills on the western face of the valley. Michael pointed to the panoramic southern horizon. "You can see the snow cap of Kilimanjaro this morning. It's almost two hundred miles away. All of those blue mountains in the foreground are the dormant volcanoes of northern Tanzania."

Doug took out his camera. "I can never capture this on film," he said as he checked his lens apertures. "It's like we're the only people left on the earth."

Margaret walked over to sit on a large rock and gazed off into the distance, overwhelmed by the vastness of the landscape. She felt herself diminished by the boundless sky, dwarfed by the ancient mighty powers that had wrenched this land apart and hurled up the mountainous rock to spew the bowels of the earth to the surface. And yet, in a curious way, she also felt herself a part of this creation because the same Creator had made her too. He had made her in His image, and she could stand upon this rift, view it, evaluate its origins, and gain a sense of her own worth, an intelligent individual in the midst of all this splendour.

Reflecting upon her discovery, she climbed into the back seat again and watched Michael carefully manoeuvre the vehicle down a staircase of geological faults on the side of the escarpment to the floor, a mile below. The coolness of the high veldt evaporated in the furnace of the valley. The harsh, stark landscape seemed like a combination of the lunar surface, and the mesas and canyons of an old western movie. As they jolted along a dusty road, Margaret wondered if the place was inhabited until they came to a large factory spewing out a fine white dust.

"Lake Magadi," Michael said.

"Where?" Doug asked.

Michael pointed to a flat white surface behind the building. "Come on. I'll show you."

The heat hit them like a blast furnace as they climbed out of the Rover and sought the shade of the Magadi Soda Company building. A workman came over to speak to Michael briefly and left again. They walked over to the edge of the lake and sifted the mixture through their fingers. "It's potash and salt among other chemicals too," Michael explained. "It's called trona. When it's refined,they use it to make glass and detergents. It's Kenya's largest mineral export. They ship it up the valley to the rail terminal and it goes from there to Mombasa."

They climbed back into the air-conditioned jeep and drove slowly along Lake Magadi past a residential area designed for the employees of the Soda Company. Near the edge of the road, Michael pointed to a small grove of bare trees. "There's a couple of gerenuk," he said slowing down. Two creatures resembling antelope stood on their hind legs, nibbling at the top branches. "They're an oddity," Michael said. "They seldom graze on all fours."

At the far end of the lake they came to an area of open water where large springs bubbled near the shore, and got out of the car again to look at the springs. Doug's shoes sank in the foul muck as he bent down to touch the water. "Wow! That's hot." His touch disturbed a group of tiny fish and he shook his head, amazed that anything could live in the hot brine.

As the sun rose higher, they drank water from the thermos jugs and headed back past Lake Magadi to pick up the road across the valley and up the western escarpment. Margaret bit her lip at times, wondering if the car would make it up the steep inclines, and Doug turned around to smile at her when he felt apprehensive himself about the rough terrain.

They finally came out onto an immense rolling plain with stands of cedar forest. Michael pulled in beneath a grove of trees and they stretched their legs again and ate the lunch Mwangi had prepared. Swarms of flies appeared from nowhere and they spent most of the meal swatting themselves and swooshing flies from the food. Unable to stand it any longer, they packed up and drank their tea as they jolted along the track toward a tarmac road into the Maasai Mara Game Preserve. Leaving the hilly escarpment they reached the wide grasslands of the Serengeti-Mara stretching far to the western horizon of blue hills. The savanna shimmered in the heat of early afternoon and any distant herds of wildebeest or antelope or zebra were lost in the glaring light.

Eventually they entered the National Park, paid their fee, received an information booklet containing the rules for tourists in their own vehicles, and headed south toward Keekerok Lodge where they had reservations for the night. As the afternoon wore on, some game became visible, wildebeest with their large heads, small horns, spindly torsos and legs; an antlered impala with his large harem of dainty consorts. Two zebra were rolling about on the side of the road luxuriating in a dust bath. As the Land Rover drew near they sprang to their feet and ran, their distinctive black and white rump patterns an arabesque pirouetting amid the low shrubs and tufts of grass. Farther away from the gate, the road became more rutted and Michael swerved several times to avoid pot-holes one of which Doug swore was deep enough to conceal a large sleeping dog. Wearied by the trip, Margaret was relieved to see the roof of an old colonial inn through the trees. She couldn't have cared less that directly behind the hotel lay several scruffy buildings serving no apparent purpose. She climbed out of the back seat and groaned as she straightened her spine. "I think a massage therapist could make a fortune in a place like this," she said as Michael hauled their bags out of the rear door.

Doug rubbed her shoulders lightly. "I'll give you a massage tonight," he said.

They registered at the desk which belonged to another time-period and discovered they were to share a room. "I hope you don't mind, Margaret," Michael said. "It's the height of the season and even though I made reservations, it's all that's available."

"Of course I don't mind," she replied. "A bed anywhere will be wonderful."

The sagging mattresses on the narrow double bed and the cot in the corner didn't look comfortable at all but she realized it was the best they could do. They barely had time to stow their gear before it was time to climb into a tourist bus and head off to the bush for some viewing. Jolting along a dusty track to a grove above a wide plain, the bus stopped. The guide cranked a handle and the ceiling of the bus slid open to expose the sky. The tourists stood on their seats as the sun sank lower behind the western cloudy horizon flooding the countryside with yellow light, illuminating the herds of grazing animals. The earth seemed to grow very still. The wildebeests lifted their heads and listened for a snapping twig. The impala startled at the shadow of a large bustard overhead. It seemed as if they were all waiting for something, someone. The tourists stood immobile, warned that the slightest cough or movement could frighten the herd into a stampede. The shadows lengthened across the quiet land. And then death arrived on padded feet. The tourists watched as three lionesses appeared from the direction of the grove. They circled their prey and in a horrorifying moment sprang into the midst of the herd selecting their victims. Hooves pounded in the dust, frantically evading the hunters. The watchers strained their eyes against the setting sun's rays. As the cloud of dust dissipated in the wisp of the evening breeze, they could see two wildebeest lying on the ground, mute in the throes of death. And in the silence of the evening, growls rumbled from the grove as more of the pride emerged to feast.

They feasted themselves that night on what was supposed to be beef, but Michael was sure was wildebeest. The liveried attendants served them a four course meal on the screened porch of the hotel. A small oil-lamp sat in the center of each table providing only enough light for the diners. Margaret thought it was a romantic touch until Michael pointed out that too much light attracted wild-life to the lodge. As they ate their meal it became quite obvious that he was right. Ringing the lodge were glowing embers, pairs of bright eyes reflecting the visible light. White moths crashed against the screen, fluttering frantically to reach the table lights, dying in drifts on the sills. Exhausted by the rigours of their long day, the Parkers went to bed, Michael to the cot in the corner, Doug and Margaret lying in a heap in the small bed.

Their accommodations the following night at Mara Serena Lodge were luxurious in comparison to the Keekerok. They had risen early because the beds were too uncomfortable to lie in once the anaesthesia of sleep had worn off. Breakfast had been served by the same liveried waiters, silver salvers on white linen. The coffee was the only redeeming feature to the tinned fruit, the hard rolls, the rubbery eggs and the burnt bacon. Hot and strong, the brew gave the tourists a sense of vitality and they set off to the wilds of the savanna in various tour buses and vans and private transport. Michael made tracks through Africa that day as they crossed the plains toward the Tanzanian border searching for the annual migration. "We're lucky," he said. "Normally it doesn't start until the first part of March. This year, the 'short rains' weren't as heavy down south and the diminished pasture has forced the herds north earlier. If the wildebeests had a choice, they would opt to stay south on the Serengeti where there are no trees, no hiding places for predators. The soil there is mostly a volcanic ash which has formed such a hard base that tree roots can't penetrate, leaving the entire plain to shallow-rooted grasses. But after they've mowed the grass to a stubble, they're forced to migrate. One old bull sniffs the air and ambles off toward Lake Victoria and more than a million wildebeests and about a quarter of a million zebras follow."

Before they reached their night's lodgings, they had seen the living river of hooves and hides pass before them. The overwhelming spectacle stretched from the southern horizon, fanning out across the plain, reaching the banks of the Talek River. Michael parked the jeep and they watched thousands of animals fording the shallow river that flowed southward from the hills on the western side of the Rift Valley. They watched the cows searching for their young, crossing back into the river again while their calves were trampled on the bank by the masses and left to die of starvation or be eaten by the preying hyenas or vultures. Close to the border they found a suitable ford and crossed the river themselves, heading for the higher ground in the north-western section of the park. The Mara Serena Lodge seemed out of place in the park. It's bright facade, clean foyer, luxurious rooms with hot showers were a dream come true to the weary Parkers who arrived at sunset.

Almost too tired to enjoy dinner and the evening entertainment of African music and dancing, Margaret said goodnight to the men and left them to visit in the dining room while she retired to the comfort of a western bed. Awakened at sunrise, they were driven out to the banks of the Mara River and the home of a large pride of black-maned lions. The old male must have known his days were numbered as several of his off-spring were almost as large as he was and there was a great deal of snarling and growling when the safari bus approached the lair. The females segregated themselves from the fray, lying about in small groups with cubs at their sides. The bus driver took them a short distance past the river and quickly pointed to a tawny blur of a cheetah streaking across the open veldt in pursuit of an evasive gazelle. The swift quarry dodged and eluded the hunter several times but the persistent hunter drove the prey to ground and the game ended. Returning to the hotel for breakfast, the bus came upon a group of giraffe feeding in a grove of acacia trees. The stately creatures moved slowly to the other side of the grove as the bus circled the area. They checked out of the hotel after breakfast, following the Mara River course north to the western corner of the reserve. Throughout the morning they came upon pools in the river where hippopotamus lay submerged in the tepid water. Bad tempered, short-sighted Cape buffalo with curled horns waded shoulder deep in the swampy shallows. Antelope too numerous to count grazed nearby. As they drove onto higher grassland, the wildebeests and zebra continued the trek north, stalked by the ever-ravenous lioness, her hungry cubs nearby. Margaret's and Doug's memories of the journey blurred as they saw different kinds of grazing animals accompanied by the predators and scavengers. Often in the distance, hawks and vultures circled in the sky, or they passed heaps of bleached bones by the track, the cycle of life continuing as it had for thousands of years.

As they left the Preserve, they came upon several Maasai herding their cattle along the road. The men bore only a vague similarity to the warriors they had seen several days before in the Bomas of Nairobi. Their dirty, ragged clothing hung loosely about their shoulders. Braided red hair hung down their backs. Empty ear lobes stretched below their jawbones. Their calloused bare feet scuffed the dust and they all seemed terribly weary. As the car approached a town at the intersection of several roads, Michael pulled into a gas station. Doug and Margaret climbed out and went over to buy a bottled soft drink and stand in the shade. A Maasai walked down the street his head held high, laughing as he passed his friends, stopping to shake their hands. His woman walked behind him, her body bent under a load of household goods. The leather strap which secured the load to her back, crossed the front of her shaven head, the imprint buried in her forehead. A young child perched on top of the load. The woman followed her husband down the street, unable to see anything except the backs of his heels. Margaret nudged Doug and grimaced. "I think I've seen enough of Kenya," she said softly.

He glanced at Michael walking toward them. "Don't say anything, dear. He's trying so hard to give us a good time."

By the time they had driven north and dropped down into the Kedong Valley, Michael turned to Margaret and asked, "How about a cup of tea? We can stop for a bit of Maasai dancing at Mayer's Farm. It's quite a tourist attraction."

She smiled brightly at him. "That sounds like fun. And a cup of tea would be nice too. What do you think, Doug?"

He reached over the back of his seat and squeezed her hand. "Sounds okay to me, Michael."

Driving past the craters of two huge old volcanoes on the valley floor they came to Mayer's Farm which was crowded with tour buses from Nairobi. They found a seat in the shade and enjoyed an English afternoon tea in the company of Japanese, Chinese, South Africans and Europeans as the ancient tribal rites of a dying race were paraded before the rising scions of the brave new world.

Climbing the eastern wall of the valley, they drove another thirty miles into Nairobi and as Michael pulled into the driveway late in the afternoon, he sighed "Now you've had a little taste of Kenya."

Doug reached over and squeezed his shoulder. "Thanks Son. We really appreciate you taking the time to show us around, don't we, Margaret."

She leaned forward to echo Doug's thanks. "And I appreciate Dorian letting you go off with us too. I'm sure she and Julianne missed you."

Dorian and the little girl had come out to the porch and Julianne was now running toward the car. Michael caught her up in his arms and they had a happy reunion as Lulu helped carry some of the bags and hampers into the house. Mwangi had prepared dinner in anticipation of their return, and after the travellers had bathed and changed their clothing, they sat at the table to eat and talk long into the evening.

"You have a day to rest," Michael said. "It's off to Mombasa bright and early Friday morning."

Dreading another long safari, Doug and Margaret were surprised to find themselves in the comfortable back seat of the Fiat whizzing along a busy highway toward the coast. Sisal plantations, rows of the sharp bladed rosettes stretched for miles beside the road. Descending from the plateau, they watched zebra and impala grazing on the tawny green grass as the morning sun trailed their long shadows across the treeless veldt. Dorian pointed to Kilimanjaro in the distance. "And ahead, on your right, are the world's youngest mountains," she added.

Doug and Margaret looked out upon a range of emerald velvet hills. "They're awfully green," Doug said. "They look so unusual in this part of the country."

"That's because of their underground rivers," Michael said. "About thirty miles south of here they erupt at Mzima Springs, about seven or eight million gallons of fresh water an hour. Mombasa gets its water from there. We'll stop at the springs on the way home."

They ate lunch at a lodge near Voi on the southern edge of Tsavo National Park and continued on through increasing traffic to the causeway leading to Mombasa Island. As Michael maneuvered the car through the dense traffic of the port city, they could see the maze of narrow side streets, almost impassable to automobiles. Mombasa seemed to be a sailor's town, bars and brothels, and a curious mixture of Arabs and Indians, with mosques, temples and shops. They drove under one of the two huge sets of crossed steel elephant tusks on Moi Avenue. "This was built to commemorate the visit of Princess Elizabeth in 1952. She became the Queen on that trip," Dorian said.

"I remember that," Margaret mused. "Wasn't she at a place called Treetops when her father died?"

"That's right," Doug said. "She went up a princess and came down a queen."

Still heading east, Michael crossed the Nyali Bridge to Freretown, and shortly after three o'clock, pulled in to the parking lot of the Whitesands Hotel at Bamburi Beach on the Indian Ocean.

The heat and humidity struck them like a hot wet towel as they emerged from the car. Within minutes, their cotton clothing clung to their bodies and they looked about for a porter to help with the luggage. "It's still siesta time," Michael said picking up some of the bags to walk into the open spacious lobby. "I hope the front desk isn't closed down too."

Their adjoining rooms on the second floor overlooked the pool and the ocean. As Doug set their bags down on the floor he tore off his shirt and lay down across the bed. Margaret walked out to the balcony to watch the waterfall flowing from one pool to another in the center of a palm studded garden. Dorian walked out on to their balcony and joined her. "What's your husband doing?" she asked.

Margaret gestured toward the room. "He's stretched out on the bed with his shirt off."

Dorian laughed. "Come and look at this," she said. Margaret peeked around the corner of the door and saw the replica of Doug also lying flat on his back. The two women laughed again. "I think I'm ready for a swim," Dorian said.

"Me too. Give me a call when you're ready to go," Margaret replied.

When she went back into the room, Doug was waiting for her. "Come on over here for a minute," he said, patting the bed beside him.

She smiled. "Not now, dear. Dorian wants to go swimming."

"Dorian can wait a few minutes, can't she. Who's more important, Dorian or me?"

She pulled her damp blouse over her head. "You are, dear. Always you . . ."

It seemed to take Dorian a long time to get ready for the beach too, and Margaret realized Doug and Michael were more alike than ever. The couples spent the rest of the afternoon bobbing about in the warm surf and lounging in the shade of the casuarinas and palms on the fine white sand. Huge cascades of bougainvillea spilled over the walkways near the hotel. White camellias blossomed amid the dark glossy leaves, and bowers of pink and white oleander grew as a hedge between the Whitesands and the Lodge next door.

They dined that evening on a sea-food menu, prawns, lobster, and a variety of local fish and rice dishes. The luminous stars hung low in the black night over the Indian Ocean, and as Doug leaned back in his chair on the flower-filled terrace, surrounded by the smell of jasmine, he thought that if he died right then, he couldn't complain. He had had a wonderful life, and now he was happier than he had ever dreamed it possible. He caught Margaret's hand. "I think I need to go for a walk." he said. "I'm stuffed to the gills with all this fish."

Michael smiled at his father. "We'd better all go together. There's safety in numbers, Dad."

"Could we be mugged?"

"I think the hotel security is okay but there aren't any guarantees. And leopards prowl at night too."

"It's hard to imagine a leopard in a lovely place like this," Margaret said.

"They were becoming an endangered species until several years ago when an international treaty banned all commerce in their fur. Now they're recovering quite well, even in populated areas. I heard about a leopard at one of the lodges up the road here. He dragged off a waiter by the head."

"Michael!" Dorian stared at her husband.

"The other waiters beat him off with sticks and he's going to be all right except for a few scars."

"I don't think I want to go for a walk, Doug," Margaret said.

"We'll be all right," Michael interjected. "We'll take the beach, away fro m overhanging trees."

The thoughts of ravenous leopards could not dispel the magic of the beach at night. The surf seemed phosphorescent at times, and as the two barefoot couples strolled hand in hand, a slight breeze blew the humidity of the day away. Later, they slept soundly beneath the mosquito netting around their beds as the waves rolling in from the ocean crashed on the reef offshore.

They went sailing the next day on a fourteen foot Laser amid windsurfers who careened about on the winds out of the northeast, free of concern for sharks since the reef was a natural barrier. Arab dhows motored out to the reef, looking for the gaps to continue their journeys across thousands of miles of ocean. "Two hundred years ago, those boats would have been loaded with blacks, headed for the slave markets of the world," Dorian said. "Perhaps my ancestors were on board."

Doug glanced at Margaret and Michael.

Michael reached over to touch her hand. "I'd have never met you, Dorian, if they hadn't. I'd probably still be in New Lancaster wondering what the rest of the world was all about."

"And we wouldn't have the most beautiful grand-daughter in the world," Doug added. He cut the motor and hauled up the sail. "And if it weren't for those Arabs inventing the lateen, we wouldn't be sailing today."

They tacked about ten miles up the coast, coming close to the reef several times where the blue-green water piled up over the coral and burst into crests of foam. Michael knew very little about sailing. As Doug attempted to teach him, Margaret said "If and when you come to visit this summer, Dorian, we'll take you sailing on a real boat. The Pretty Lady is Doug's pride and joy."

"So you're a sailor too," Dorian mused.

"I haven't had a lot of experience," Margaret admitted. "But I love being on the boat with Doug . . . The two of us together combating the elements of nature . . . I think sailing develops a bond between two people, dependence and survival."

They came back to the hotel jetty on a fast run before the noreaster. The sun was becoming so hot they took a fast dip in the ocean and went inside to shower and change before lunch in the garden. Dorian peered up into the large shade tree. "Just checking for wildlife," she said to Michael who had frowned at her.

Margaret smiled. "I think Kenya must be a mecca for birdwatchers," she said. "I've never seen so many different species."

"I don't know anything about birds," Doug said, "but I would guess a lot of these have migrated from Europe and Central Asia for the winter."

"I think you're right, Dad. I've heard of groups of people who come to Kenya to look at the butterflies. They can see elephants and giraffes in the zoo, but insects are their passion."

"To each his own," Dorian said. "A lot of tourists come to Kenya for the deep-sea fishing. They're in pursuit of the mythical marlin, those thousand pound beasts just beyond the reef. They return home satisfied with the huge ocean perch or yellow tuna. Someday I'd like to go to the marine parks north of here. I hear the sights of fish and coral are absolutely beautiful."

"Wait until Margaret and I come back the next time, Dorian," Doug said. "We'll put that on the top of our list of things to do."

They drove that afternoon a short distance up the coast to the Bamburi Cement Factory. Michael explained that the coral limestone lying under much of Kenya's coastal plain was now exported to the Arabian peninsula, a significant boon to the country's trade deficit. They saw evidences of the commerce in the unsightly scars left behind on the surface, huge quarries gaping in the hot sun. Michael drove on through a forest of pine and oak, across the green meadows of a small wildlife park, a banana plantation and a vineyard, to a large crocodile farm. As they got out of the car to view the ugly creatures, somnolent on the shady bank, Michael explained that this was once part of the cement factory too. "The experts had said that nothing could be done with the land," he explained. "It was too saline to support vegetation. The owners of the factory felt they couldn't sacrifice the land for the profits they were reaping from the cement business so they hired a Swiss fellow to see what he could do. Rene Haller rehabilitated the environment so successfully that now scientists come from all over the world to see the results."

"It's comforting to know that big business feels some accountability to the environment," Doug said. "I wonder if they'll do something for the Brazilian rain forest."

They dined that night in Mombasa at the Capri, an air-conditioned, candlelit restaurant in an old hotel. After an excellent feast of seafood, they strolled over to the veranda of the Castle Hotel for dessert and drinks to watch the ladies of the town parade the street in search of clients for the evening. The Saturday night crowd filled the bars with raucous laughter and the clink of glasses, barely heard above the music, a mixture of western jazz and eastern drums and scithar.

They checked out of the hotel the next morning after an early walk on the beach at low tide, a mosaic of rocky pools teeming with stranded small fry and scuttling crabs. Driving back toward Mombasa, they passed the brooding hulk of Fort Jesus, the symbol of Portuguese colonialism. Cathedral bells and Muslim recordings on towers called the faithful to prayer in Mombasa as the town struggled to its feet after the orgies of the previous evening.

Michael drove back to the same restaurant at Voi for brunch before they swung off the main road, and crossing the Taita Hills, entered Tsavo National Park, a land of rocky hills and gullies, and red sand drifts. The road seemed in a tolerable state for travel but curved around obstacles such as huge termite mounds and outcroppings of volcanic rock, plunging into ravines and rising again over barren heaths. Old trees lay scattered across the landscape, their trunks and branches bleached white in the sun like old bones in a vandalized graveyard.

"It's the elephants," Michael explained. "There was a terrible drought here several years ago and migrating herds were desperate for water. The damage they did to this part of the park was almost irreparable. Eventually, the park manager culled the herd, and between the drought and poaching for the ivory, the numbers were significantly reduced."

They drove on toward the northwest and came upon grazing herds. An ostrich lifted its head from the sand and pounded after the car. "Why?" Doug asked in amazement as he pointed his camera at the awkward bird with the long neck and tiny head keeping pace with the Fiat for almost a mile.

"This one looks like it got separated from the main flock and thinks we're part of his family," Michael replied.

The bird tired and slowed to a brisk trot, disappearing in the trail of dust. "There's Kilimanjaro," Michaell said, nodding his head to the southwest. Clouds were beginning to form halfway up the mountain but the snow cap was still visible. The hills were becoming larger now with fordable streams and more jungle like vegetation. Monkeys and birds filled the trees. Any animals were obscured by the dense growth along the road. Michael slowed the car and pointed to a dark mass in the undergrowth. "There's a rhino," he said.

Doug grabbed his camera. "It's too dark," he murmured. "I can't see him. Can I get out and go a little closer?"

"Not if you value your life," Michael replied. "They can get pretty nasty. Roll down the window and I'll drive past very slowly. Perhaps you can get a shot from behind."

As the Fiat crept along the road it became clear that this was a rhinoceros with a young calf. The near-sighted creature lifted its horned snout and moved toward the car. "That's the fella," Doug whispered. "Just a little more and I've got you . . . Hey. Not so fast! Michael! He's charging the car!"

"What the . . ." Michael swung his head around to look and at the same time accelerated. The car leaped forward as the rhino's horn grazed the bumper.

Dorian was on her knees in the front seat staring out the rear window. "Can't this car go any faster?" she shouted.

"I'm doing forty!" Michael yelled. "Do you want me to turn it over in the ditch?"

Margaret bit her lip and squeezed Doug's hand as she watched the beady eyes sunken in the huge head.

Doug patted Michael's shoulder. "I think we're losing him. He's falling behind."

"It's not a him, Dad. It's a mother. Did you get your picture?"

"I think so. With all the fuss, I may have got a good shot of a tree instead."

They pulled into Mzima Springs and watched the huge geyser formed by the underground rivers to the north. The main attraction was the hippo jacuzzi. The hippopotamuses wallowing in the pools were viewed from a platform, or at snout level from the bank or through the windows of a bunker. Crocodiles amicably occupied the same premises.

They left Tsavo and drove on to the Amboseli Park. Kilimanjaro loomed closer now as they followed the track into the heartland of former Maasai country. The only native peoples to be seen had washed off the red paint, cut off their hair and now sold beads and swords, or served food to the tourists at the lodges in the park. They stopped for a meal in the late afternoon and watched the vultures soaring on the hot up-drafts over the deserted plain. The winds sweeping in from the Indian Ocean formed thermal currents, drawing the dust into whirling columns that rushed across the floor of the veldt, sweeping everything in its path. Small birds, trapped in its power, were flung lifeless to the ground miles away from the trees where they had nested.

Driving on through a swampy area where fresh water bubbled up through fissures in the black lava, they came upon a great number of white egrets accompanying a herd of buffalo. Bold ox-peckers sat on the shoulders and haunches of the beasts as they wallowed in the marshy grass. Breaking through the thickets they came onto a flat desert surrounding Lake Amboseli, now a mere puddle surrounded by a large pan of saline dust.

"It fills up in the rainy season," Michael explained.

"It looks like it's full now," Doug said.

"It's a mirage, Dad."

Doug sat up to stare out the front window. "It can't be," he said looking out at the liquid horizon. "I can even see the reflections of that herd of wildebeests in the water . . ."

Michael drove toward the mirage which moved further away. They reached the herd and passed it by on dry land. Doug shook his head. "It seemed so real," he said.

"Kenya is an illusion," Dorian said quietly. "What began as a model for Africa with Kenyatta is becoming now a burdensome society. The native people are poorer than before in many ways, and with the pressures of modernization, I wonder if there is a place for them at all. The statistics show a black woman will give birth to eight children and now Kenya can only afford to educate one of them. It seems hopeless, doesn't it."

"And my job," Michael added, "is to figure out how to feed this growing population as we enter a new millennium."

Doug laid his hand on Margaret's knee. "It makes life in New Lancaster seem pretty simple, doesn't it. And at our age, I guess it isn't our problem anymore."

They reached the north gate of the park at sunset and saw the one sight that every tourist to Kenya dreams about at night. Kilimanjaro lay on the southern horizon, its base in dark shadows, a ruff of golden cloud about its shoulders, its snow cap, red and gold against a pink and amber sky. A massive herd of elephants ambled near the shore of the dry lake, their silhouettes against the lighted background of salt beds, their shoulders and backs reflecting the golden hues of sunset.

"I've never seen anything so beautiful," Margaret breathed.

Her companions nodded their agreement, silently aware that even a word might dispel the magic that surrounded them. The shadows lengthened as the panorama faded into night. In the distance they heard the roar of a lion and knew death once more stalked on padded feet. Climbing back into the car they headed north to Nairobi. Several miles from the park, Michael saw a revolving light in the distance and slowed down as a forlorn diesel horn blared at a crossing. A long freight train of salt encrusted cars lumbered along the rails in front of them carrying produce of the Magadi Soda Company. Two hours later, they arrived home.

Lulu was watching television, Julianne was in bed, and Mwangi had gone home. While Dorian chatted with Lulu, Michael went out to the kitchen and he and Margaret and Doug made a light supper.

"It's back to work tomorrow, Dad," he said. "Have you and Margaret any plans for this week?"

"I've been thinking we might rent a car and take a ride into Uganda," Doug replied.

Dorian sipped her tea. "Are you sure you want to do that?" she asked.

"Yes. I'll rent the car tomorrow, take a trial run around town, and we could leave the middle of the week."

"I'll call a friend of mine in the morning," Michael offered. "He has a rental agency. What would you like to drive, a sedan or a land rover?"

"I think something with a lot of power," Doug said. "We don't want to get run over by any more charging rhinos."

"I'll ask Sam to drop off a vehicle for you in the morning and perhaps you'd like to take a run up to the UN for lunch with me. I'll meet you in the rotunda at the information desk at noon."

Mr. Samuel Sharma appeared on the veranda shortly after Dorian and Michael had left for work the next morning. Julianne ran around the table as Doug sat down to fill out the various forms and contracts. Mwangi was busy polishing the floor in the living room and Lulu was doing the laundry. Margaret read the road maps M.r Sharma had brought with him and realized that there was still much of Kenya to be seen. At last they were done and Mr. Sharma took them outside to show them the Range Rover he had brought with him. Handing Doug the keys, he said "And now if you will be kind enough to return me to my office . . ."

"Sure," Doug said. "Hop in."

Several minutes later he returned and threw the car keys on the bed where Margaret was reading a story to Julianne. He sat down heavily beside her. "We'll be lucky to get out of this country without being killed," he said. "I just can't get the hang of driving on the wrong side of the road. Whenever I go around a corner I end up swerving out of someone's way."

She tried to console him. "It'll be better when you're not in a lot of traffic, dear. Why don't you take Julianne and me for a drive around the neighbourhood and get used to it?"

Doug practised driving in the suburbs of Ngara that morning. They drove past the homes and gardens of Europeans, diplomats, and wealthy business people. Further afield, they came to very modest homes of Kenyans who were making their way in the world. Several school yards were full of children at play in their distinctive uniforms, mostly white blouses and shirts, and red, blue or khaki skirts and pants. Julianne enjoyed her outing with her grandparents, and cried when they took her home to Lulu for lunch and her nap. Doug and Margaret set off up Limuru Rd. and headed for their luncheon date with Michael.

The UN building was located about five miles north of Nairobi's outskirts. As Doug approached the complex he whistled. "Look at that," he said. The gleaming steel and glass buildings rose from the tawny green veldt. They stopped at a directory listing all the agencies in the fenced compound with an accompanying map stating, "You are here." He pulled ahead to the guard house where a uniformed attendant approached with a smile. When he explained he was looking for the rotunda, he was directed to the main building ahead with a large parking lot in front.

Entering the bright lobby with colourful flags hanging overhead they found the information desk, announced their arrival and sat down to watch the world go by. Michael soon appeared and led them across a vast marble rotunda to the dining room. They had not expected a small cafeteria, but they were certainly unprepared for the dining experience that awaited them. A thick carpet muted much of the noise of the crowded room. The silken tapestries on the walls added an old world elegance to the decor, as well as the snowy linen tables and deeply upholstered chairs. The maitre d 'led them to a table and gave them each a leather bound menu. A waiter appeared with a silver pitcher of ice water to fill the crystal glasses.

"How do the poor people live?" Doug murmured as he sipped his water.

Michael nodded. "I wanted you to see this so the next time you hear about the UN needing money you'll know why. I work for the organization and I know it serves a very valuable role, but there's this political mind-set about using the public purse to further your own comfort and ambition. If you look around this room, most of these people come from the third world, and yet once they get a taste of power, it's very easy to forget your roots and join the club."

"Are you happy here, Son?" Doug asked.

Michael stared at him for a moment. "No," he admitted. "I'm not happy. After seeing the poverty in the rural communities where I do most of my work, I don't think I'll ever be happy again. I'm not sure any of us ever has the right to be happy while there's suffering and hunger. I grew up in a land of make-believe. You and Mom gave me an idyllic childhood. But Africa's changed me. It's spoiled that fairy-tale existence and I can never go home again." He sensed his father's concern. "Don't worry about me, Dad. I may not be happy, but I do have a sense of purpose for my life, a fulfillment in seeing a job done right. I have contacts from the sub-Sahara to South Africa, and we are making a difference. Not a big difference but it's changing, a little bit at a time. Remember I showed you the Bamburi Cement Company? When we have the opportunity to work with corporate management to restore something on that magnitude then it gives all of us hope that we can right the wrongs of yesterday and have an impact on the future."

Margaret listened as Michael explained to his father some of the new projects they were working on in Tanzania and Mozambique.

By the time lunch had ended, she rose from the table with an added appreciation for her step-son.

He smiled at her as they said good-bye. "I hope I haven't bored you with all this technical mumbo-jumbo."

She touched his arm. "Of course not."

Doug seemed pre-occupied on the way home and she knew it wasn't the driving.

"So what do you really think about Michael?" she asked.

His hands gripped the steering wheel. "I wish our kids could have the kind of life we've had," he said at last. "They seem to have to deal with so many more problems than we did."

She turned to him in surprise. "Think about it for a minute. Our kids have never known anything like the dirty thirties that you and I were born into. They've never had parents or uncles or brothers go off to fight in a war. They've never lived in a time where atomic bombs were killing thousands of innocent women and children. Our children have known the best of everything. Michael says he had an idyllic childhood, and he's right. The problems I see our children facing are internal. They may have some hard times financially but the hardest thing they have to deal with is finding out who they are. I think they've got lost in all the technology. They've become numbers instead of people. And I don't think the human heart can handle that anonymity. Our ids and our egos cry out for identity, for that sense of being alive and not having lived in vain. Everyone needs to feel important to someone else. Can you imagine how you would feel if you woke up every morning knowing that there wasn't another single soul on the face of the earth who gave a tinker's dam whether you were alive or dead?"

Doug pulled the car over to the side of the road and stopped. "I can't talk and drive on the wrong side of the road at the same time." He turned sideways on the seat. "So what are you really saying? What are you trying to tell me?"

Margaret shrugged. "I don't know. Since we left home, things have been different. We're tired. We've been so busy . . . Sometimes I feel far away from God. I haven't read the Bible since I got here. I look at these poor people and I know there's nothing I can do to help them. I feel lost. I've sort of become a spectator on life. I'm on the outside looking in . . ."

He reached out to touch her cheek. "Perhaps we shouldn't have come."

"Oh no," she replied quickly. "I wouldn't have missed all this for the world. God is using this to teach me something. I don't know what yet, but when I find out, it'll be worth it."

Doug touched her cheek. "You know what I think . . . I miss us being together, alone. Talking together like this. About the only time I've seen you alone lately is in bed."

She smiled. "That's true."

He turned around and started the engine. "Let's get out of here tomorrow. We'll stock up on some food and water and head off to see the sights ourselves. Now, how to I find that store where Dorian bought the milk?"

They left Nairobi early the next morning before Michael and Dorian went off to work. Michael hugged his father. "Now you've got our telephone numbers at home and work, and if you run into any trouble, be sure to call us right away." Doug grinned at Dorian. "Talk about role reversal. I seem to remember saying the same things to him when I sent him off to school."

"That was Guelph. This is Africa."

Dorian hugged Margaret. "Have a good time and stay close to civilization."

They set off up the Uhuru Highway, the road map on Margaret's knees. About five miles north of Nairobi they turned on to side road across flat grassland that stretched to the eastern horizon. Mount Kenya rose against the northern brilliant blue sky, its snows the colour of strawberry ice cream amid the glistening glaciers. As they drove across the veldt the sky faded to turquoise and then to a paler hue. As they drew closer to the massive mountain, scrubby thorns and acacias gave way to huge camphor trees and ficus and African figs whose spreading branches resembled evergreens. The forest growth became so dense with vines that it became impossible to see the trees. "Now I know where that expression came from," laughed Margaret.

The road wound higher up the mountain and broke through the jungle wall to an alpine forest. Nestled on the slope amid immaculately manicured gardens lay the Mount Kenya Safari Club Resort. "I'll see if they have a vacancy," Doug said.

"But it's the middle of the morning," Margaret said.

He grinned and climbed out of the car. "Can you think of a nicer place for us to be alone together?"

She knew the accommodations were expensive as soon as she saw the sunken jacuzzi on their balcony overlooking the pool and golf course. They lunched on the terrace amid a glittering crowd of the rich and famous. Doug found himself sitting beside a man at the next table. He leaned over to whisper to Margaret, "If I didn't know better, I'd swear that was Arnold Palmer."

She leaned around to look. "I think you're right. Why don't you ask him? All he can do is say no."

Doug wiped his mouth with the pink linen napkin. "Excuse me," he said. "Are you Arnold Palmer?"

The rugged looking man turned around and smiled. "And who wants to know?"

Doug stuck out his hand. "Doug Parker, from Canada."

"Arnie Palmer, US of A. So what's a poor Canuck doing in a place like this?" he asked.

Doug nodded to Margaret and introduced her. "We're visiting family in Nairobi."

"You wouldn't happen to be a golfer, would you, Doug? We're looking for a fourth man for this afternoon."

Doug hesitated and Margaret said, "He loves to play golf."

Arnie wiped his chin and said, "Tee off time is one-thirty. We'd like to have you join us. Billy Casper and Nick Faldo and I came over to play the Kenya Open in a couple of weeks. Jack was supposed to come too but something came up . . . Have you got your clubs with you?"

"No," Doug replied.

"The pro shop will look after you," Arnie said. He stood up. "I'll go and find those guys and tell them we're all set."

Doug collapsed in his chair. "Margaret," he said weakly. "What have you done? I'm no match for those guys. They're pro's. I'm going to look like a fool beside them."

"So what," she grinned. "It's just a game. And if they haven't played here before either then you'll all be in the same boat."

"But we're supposed to be spending the day together, remember?"

She laughed. "You can spend tonight with me instead. Don't disappoint Arnie. He's looking forward to having you along."

"But what will you do this afternoon?"

"I'll write postcards and go for a swim. I need a manicure, my hangnail is bothering me. Don't worry, dear. Just wait until you tell Ed and the boys at the club that you played golf with the celebrities."

She was getting ready to get in the jacuzzi after a bracing swim when the door to their room opened. Doug came in grinning from ear to ear. He came over to kiss her and she said, "You look like the cat that swallowed the canary. What happened?"

"I had a terrific afternoon, just couldn't do anything wrong. I think they tried to be gentle with me at first, but when I started sinking twenty and thirty foot putts, they took off the gloves and I still beat them." He stripped off his clothes and climbed into the jacuzzi too. "It was funny because before we started, they asked me if I wanted to play for ten bucks a hole, and I said `No. I didn't want to take all their money.' On the eighteenth hole, Arnie asked me if all the amateurs in New Lancaster played like me, so I invited him up to see."

"You invited Arnold Palmer to New Lancaster!"

"Sure. I don't think he'll ever come but wouldn't it be a hoot if he did."

They chuckled over the events of the day as they sat on the balcony in the warm water and watched the sun setting on the glaciers above their heads. As they dressed for dinner in their simple clothing, they wondered if there was a dress code for the dining room. The wealthy patrons of the prestigious Club shared eclectic tastes. Silken gowns, black ties and tails mingled freely among khaki safari suits and boots. During and after dinner, as the orchestra played waltzes and show tunes, Doug and Margaret danced with royalty, film stars, and heirs of the world's fortunes. As they spun past a table of three tired golfers, Arnie raised his glass and smiled.

They circled Mount Kenya the next morning driving through bamboo forests at a higher elevation and came down the other side into "Elsa" country. They stopped several places to watch the zebra, oryx and the blue-shanked ostrich. As the day wore on they realized if they were to reach Tree Tops before sundown, they would have to hurry. Unfortunately, several tour buses had arrived and Doug and Margaret were forced to find accommodation in a small lodge nearby. They were able to watch the floodlit scene at the waterholes from a viewing platform. Elephants, lions, leopards, buffalo and waterbuck came to drink. The raucous squeals of hyena were heard amid the grunting, snarling, trumpeting throng and Margaret wondered if they were attracted by the lights because it would have made more sense for the animals to drink during the day when the competition for space was less. She learned later that the water-holes were fenced off during the day and it was only opened to benefit the owners of the hotel with the lucrative tourist trade. That revelation jaded her opinion of the tourism industry and she was quite happy when Doug suggested they head back down through the Aberdares Mountain Park to pick up the trans-African highway into Uganda.

The weather was perfect that morning as they started out after breakfast. The clear blue skies, a freshness in the air pointed to another glorious day. Cobwebs, five feet across, spanned the bushes, beaded with sparkling dew drops. As the road around the mountain led them higher, a cool mist descended and Doug turned on the heater. The day became increasingly gloomy as the vegetation along the road towered menacingly overhead, black and dripping. And then it began to rain. The road deteriorated and Doug stopped to check the map wondering if he had missed a turn. They sat in a cold silence, munching on crackers, drinking water inside while the windshield streamed with the downpour.

"I thought it wasn't supposed to rain for a few more weeks," Margaret moaned.

"Yeah, but I read somewhere that Lake Victoria has its own weather system too. And we are up a mountain," he added.

Tired of waiting, Doug started to inch his way along the track, his headlights picking the way through darkened forest. They came over a rise late in the afternoon and saw the sky lightening to the west. "We're coming out of it now, I think," he mused. She squeezed his hand. "Thank God."

The road descended down a precipitous incline and Doug fought to keep the car from skidding in the mud. They entered more jungle-like vegetation and the world grew dark again. "How big is this mountain anyway?" Doug grumbled. "It's taken us all day and we're still not back in civilization. I hope I don't run out of gas."

Margaret laughed to cheer him up. "I'm not going to swim home this time," she said.

He chuckled, remembering other days.

As the forest faded behind them and the bright sun appeared again in the western sky, Doug suddenly felt the car sliding and he turned the wheel sharply to no avail. They had slipped into the ditch. He put it into reverse and tried to back out of the predicament but the wheels spun helplessly. He tried rocking it to gain a footing but again, the vehicle was stuck. He opened the car to get out and his foot sank in a foot of thick red mud. "Try your door, dear. See if it will open."

She pushed and felt the resistance of the mud too. "What are we going to do?" she asked quietly.

He scratched his head. "I dunno. It's going to be dark before long and I don't know where we are . . . Perhaps I should walk down the road apiece and see if there's anyone around."

"I'm coming too," she said.

"You'll be safer in the car . . ."

She interrupted him. "We'll be safer if we stay together."

He nodded and released the latch on the back door. They clambered across the back seat and sprang across the mud-filled ditch to the road where Doug put on his muddy shoe. Walking a short distance down the sloping track they saw a farm house where smoke curled from the chimney. "That's a relief," Doug sighed. Hand in hand they walked down to the log and wattle house. "Hallo," Doug called as a dog rose on the threshold and watched them warily.

A short stocky black man came around the corner of the house.

"Hello," Doug said again. "We've had some trouble up the road apiece. Would you have a tractor to pull us out of the mud?"

The black man raised his eyebrows. "Sure. I get the tractor and we fix you up good."

"Thanks," Doug said. "We'll start walking back up there now."

They had almost reached the ditch when the tractor overtook them, an old Ford which wheezed and coughed its way up the hill. The farmer sized up the situation quickly, deciding it was easier to pull the car forward down the hill rather than pull it backwards up the hill. He brandished a large chain and Doug felt obligated to wade knee deep into the red chocolate butter to hook it onto the frame under the bumper. Margaret watched in chagrin as Doug sank deeper into the morass, hanging onto the grill with one hand while his other shoulder and arm disappeared in the muck.

"I think that's got it," he called at last, and stood up covered in the goo. He slowly pulled himself a foot at a time clear of the car, and the tractor sprang to life, emitting great belches of smoke and fumes. The chain strained and the car moved slightly. The tractor engine roared again and the car began to slide up the bank. Doug stood to one side, the mud dripping from his entire body. He held up his hand. "Just a minute," he called. "Here Margaret. Hop in and turn the wheels."

She waded gingerly along the bank and managed to swing herself inside the car. Eventually they were on solid ground and the farmer came back to retrieve his chain.

"Thank you," Doug said, reaching inside his vest for his wallet with sticky fingers.

The black man shook his head. "No pay. You do all the work."

Doug pulled out several pound notes. "I insist. We'd never get out of there without your help." He placed them in the man's left hand and held out his right hand. "Thank you again."

The black man shook Doug's hand. "And I, Njorge, thank you. I am sorry you and Memsaab have a bad time."

Doug smiled. "We'll be all right now."

As the tractor rumbled off down the hill, Doug stripped off his outer clothing. Margaret wadded it into a ball and they sorted out the inside of the car as Doug found something warm to wear.

They drove slowly through the tea and coffee plantations where farmers like Njorge tilled their fields, until the road descended over the edge of the fractured escarpment into the Rift Valley. A bright blue lake lay below with a pink froth along the shore. Green pastures and grain fields stretched from the far side of the lake westward up an undulating slope toward a high range of purple mountains on the distant horizon. They reached the valley floor, circled the southern flank of an extinct volcano and came to the town of Nakuru. Doug pulled into a garage and left the car to be washed and checked for mud damage while they roamed about in search of a decent place to eat. The waiter in a small hotel dining room looked very much like Njorge. They watched the man, a member of the Kikuyu tribe, serving food to the other Kenyan guests. His face with the narrow forehead, the flat nose, the receding chin, shone above his clean white kanzu. He wore a single earring and no shoes.

Margaret yawned over her second cup of coffee. "Shall we spend the night here?"

Doug grimmaced. "Not here," he said. "We'll see if we can find something a little more European."

They picked up the clean car an hour later and drove out to a lodge on Lake Nakuru where a million pink flamingos waded along the shore. Refreshed by a hot shower, they rested on the veranda that evening watching the awesome spectacle of rosy flocks arriving on the lake. The blue-green algae thrived in the alkaline waters attracting millions of the birds to the feast, which in turn attracted ornithologists to watch. Margaret and Doug watched the birders as the sun set behind the high Mau hills. Cameras flashed catching the roseate mass against the orange glow above the darkened hills. At dinner, they learned from a table companion that the flamingos migrated up and down the valley depending on the food supply in the soda lakes. "In the dry season," the birder said, "the grass becomes straw, the water evaporates from the lake and if the drought is prolonged, Nakuru can become a dust bowl. The afternoon winds raise the soda dust, making the air as opaque as a London fog." After dinner, Margaret and Doug retired early. The flamingos had already tucked their heads under their wings and slept, balanced on one leg in the shallows.

After breakfast they left for Uganda on the Trans-African Highway, climbing up the western wall of the rift. Flocks of sheep grazed on the highland plateau in the misty chill of the morning. Far to the northwest, they watched the sunrise fading on Mount Elgon, another massive extinct volcano. The European settlers had left the area years before and now the African community farmed the land, wheat and maize, beef and dairy farms, coffee plantations and on the higher ground, apple orchards. The land sloped gently toward the north shore of Lake Victoria. Doug turned onto the southern branch of the highway and crossed the border into a densely populated area into Uganda.

They encountered no difficulties with the officials and were soon heading directly west toward the city of Jinja on the Nile River. Approaching the city, Doug stopped at a gas station to inquire for directions to the Beyanatha compound. Two more stops were necessary before he found someone who recognized the name. He drove through a maze of streets along the river until he came to the Owen Falls' Electric Company and turned left up a steep incline to a large compound set among a group of jacaranda trees behind a high barbed wire fence.

"It looks like a jail," Margaret murmured as she looked at the neat rows of cement block buildings in the background of the empty front field.

Doug pulled up to the gate house and got out of the car. A man of medium height and handsome by western standards, dressed in a white shirt and kahki shorts appeared in the doorway. He smiled at Doug, his white even teeth shining in his brown face, his wide set eyes, dark and friendly. They spoke briefly and the guard pointed into the compound. Doug shook his hand and returned to the car. "It's okay," he said. "We can go in."

"Why all the security?" Margaret asked. "It's an orphanage, isn't it? Surely they don't have thieves trying to steal the children."

Doug shrugged and drove on into the compound. As they passed the large open windows, they realized some of these buildings were classrooms. Children were seated at tables inside. Doug drove on to a small building in front of a quadrangle where the Ugandan flag fluttered in the breeze. "This looks like the office," he said, parking the car under the shade tree. "Let's go and meet Mr. David Davis."

"Why on earth would anyone name a child Dave Davis?" Margaret muttered as she climbed out of the car. Uncertain of what would happen next, she followed Doug inside as he presented himself to an African woman at a desk.

She raised her large dark eyes. "May I help you?"

"We'd like to see Mr. Davis if he isn't too busy," Doug said.

She waited.

"We're from Canada," Doug explained. "We know his brother and we said we'd look him up while we're here."

"Reverend Davis is at the hospital," she said. "I don't know when he'll be back in the office."

"Oh." Doug turned to Margaret. "What should we do? Wait for him? Or should we look for a place to spend the night?"

Margaret exhaled slowly. "I don't know, dear. Perhaps we could wait for a few minutes anyway."

Doug turned back to the desk. "Would you mind if we waited for him? We could sit outside under the tree."

The woman shrugged her shoulders. "I'll tell him you're here when he comes back."

They wandered outside to look for a place to sit in the shade. A large building stood across the square and there seemed to be several benches nearby. As they drew closer to the building, Margaret said "I think this is the hospital she was talking about. Isn't that a red cross over the door?"

"You're right. We'll just sit down and wait for him to come out."

"But you don't know what he looks like . . ."

"We know his brother. Maybe there'll be a family resemblance."

Several minutes later as they sat in the shade, a tall thin white man emerged from the building. He paused outside and reached in a pocket for a handkerchief to blow his nose. As they watched him wipe his eyes, he turned and saw them. He stared for a moment and then walked toward them. Doug stood up and held out his hand. "Reverend Davis, I presume . . ."

David Davis smiled. "You sound like Stanley greeting Livingston," he said.

"I'm Doug Parker, and this is my wife, Margaret. We know your brother Dan. We live near Englewood back in Canada."

He reached down to shake Margaret's hand, his thin tired face wreathed in a smile. "So you know Dan!"

"I met your nephew Jeff at camp last summer. He's a wonderful boy, isn't he. He tells me he's going to come and help you when he's bigger."

David sighed. "I could sure use some help about now."

Doug laid a hand on his shoulder. "Is there anything we can do?"

David glanced at him. "Not really. We're chronically short of help everywhere, . . . the kitchen, the school, the hospital. We just lost a two-year old girl a few minutes ago."

Doug frowned. "She died? What was the problem?"

David Davis turned to him and said wearily. "You don't know about this place then, do you."

"What do you mean?" Doug asked.

David motioned him to sit down and he sat down beside them, stretching his long bony legs out in front. "Beyanatha is a children's center for AIDS victims. There are almost twelve million Africans infected by the virus and a catastrophe of unimaginable proportions is looming on the horizon. And so many of these victims are women and children. Women have little or no knowledge of the disease and are the most vulnerable. And so when a woman in this district, dies of `slim disease' and there is no family willing to help, her children are brought here. Some of her older children may be free of the virus, but the younger ones, especially the suckling infants are doomed." He passed his hands across his face. "Little Wangari just died, and now I have to tell her older sister Wanjiru."

Margaret moistened her lips. "Do these girls have a father?"

"Every child has a father. But no one knows where this one is. He may be dead himself. Or he may be driving a truck along the Trans-African Highway infecting every woman in sight. This problem isn't going to go away until they find a cure for the disease. The African continent has millions of sexually active youth who are ticking time bombs. A whole generation is in danger of extinction. And it doesn't help when the white races in the UN vote against supplying funds for more education and prevention of the disease."

Doug shook his head. "You must get awfully discouraged working in a place like this."

David nodded. "It would be easy to give up," he admitted. "But the name on the gate is Beyanatha, Haven of Hope, and the only hope for this world is found in Jesus Christ, so it doesn't really matter whether I serve Him here or someplace else." He sat up straight. "So what are you people doing in Africa?"

"My son and his family live in Kenya. When Dan told us about you, we decided to drive over and say hello. So here we are."

Margaret touched his arm. "You say you're short of staff? Is there anyone else from Canada here working with you?"

"There are two nurses in the hospital from Toronto and a teacher from Alberta in the school. We depend on a doctor from Jinja to treat the children. Most of the workers are local Christians. And students from an American Bible College come in the summer to help with the maintenance and repairs." He rubbed his face. "We all get tired though, really tired. I'm afraid Judy and Marion, the nurses are getting burned out. Their assistants try to take some of the load but the responsibility still falls on their shoulders." He stood up. "Come and let me show you around."

He led them back into the hospital where rows of cribs and beds lined the walls. Wasted toddlers lay against the white sheets, their skin grey and their dark eyes sunken, too weak to cry. Margaret stood beside one of the cribs and touched a little hand. The fingers curled gently around hers and she leaned down to stroke the sparse wiry hair from the brow. The child's eyes watched her listlessly. Margaret smelled the baby had soiled its diaper. She found a pile of clean diapers and wipes, and so she quickly changed the baby. Dan Davis walked toward the end of the ward and reluctantly, Margaret turned the baby on her side and hurried after the men. She joined them in the next ward where a Canadian nurse had assembled several aides about the bed of an older child to demonstate a procedure. She listened for a moment to the woman patiently explaining the instructions before going on to join the men at the far end of the hospital. Dan was showing Doug the windowless store room where a limited supply of drugs lined the shelves. "Theft is one of our biggest problems," he said. "Drugs are always in demand on the black market. We have to watch the foodstores too. That's why we use the barbed wire. A chap patrols the area at night with a dog now so that seems to help."

They left the hospital and walked a short distance to the dormitories where rows of neat bunks lined the walls. An open dining area under a thatched roof, with a kitchen at one end, stood under a huge jacaranda tree. One black woman stood before a large wood stove, stirring a cauldron of mush. "It's ugale," Dan said. "A mixture of cereal and corn."

Another woman was mixing up a batch of dough for the evening's flat bread. She called out to David. "Do your friends want a cuppa?"

He turned to Doug and Margaret. "Would you like a cup of tea?"

"That would be very nice," Margaret said, smiling at the woman's offer of hospitality. She watched the woman add some tea leaves to an enamel pot and pour boiling water from a kettle on the stove. The woman brought them three white enamel mugs and added two heaping teaspoons of sugar to each before pouring the tea. She smiled as they thanked her and she went back to her task.

"That's Umendi," David explained as they sauntered across the yard toward the school. "She's been here since the school started. I don't know what I'd do without her."

Sipping the tea, they listened outside the building as the reading lesson inside continued. The children read the English words in unison. "For God so loved the world that He gave His only begotten Son . . ."

The words of the gospel passed out the large open windows onto the compound. Doug scratched his head. "The Ugandan government doesn't mind you teaching from the Bible?"

David smiled wryly. "Not yet. They aren't as enlightened as the western governments. They're glad we're here to help them, too."

They walked on to the next classroom where a math class was learning the multiplication table from a teacher with a hint of a western drawl. "This is Bill Grant's class. He's going home to be married in the spring. I thank God everyday his bride is coming back here with him to teach too."

"Are you married, Dan?" Margaret asked.

A cloud crossed his eyes briefly. "No. My fiancee died in our last year of Bible school. She had leukemia. That's why I came out here, I suppose. I just wanted to get away from everything that would remind me of her, and I've been here ever since."

He walked them past the school to a large garden at the back of the property. "After school, some of the children come back to weed and harvest the vegetables for the kitchen staff. It's good training for them and keeps them out of mischief. Samuel is the gardener who supervises them. He's probably having a siesta someplace now."

They walked along the rows in the garden, amazed at the profusion and variety of vegetables. The sweet corn seemed to be about ten feet high, two huge cobs on each stock. Tomatoes, cabbages, cauliflowers and sweet potatoes grew abundantly alongside rows of onions, carrots and beets. Pumpkin vines littered one corner with masses of flowers promising a good crop as well.

As they circled back toward the front of the property, they came to the wash house where laundry was drying on a line. Two black women were bent over tubs underneath the thatched roof, singing as they scrubbed the children's clothing. "Two more saints," David murmured. "The lavatories are next door."

He turned and gestured to the building in front of the quadrangle. "And this is the office. I have a bunk in here so this is home for me too."

"I'd like to take your picture, David, so Dan can see where you live. I'll send you a print too." Doug took several shots of the place before they said their goodbyes.

As they drove out through the gate, Doug shook his head. "What a place for a young man to be, all alone, with all those kids, and most of them dying at that. God! I'll never forget this place as long as I live!"

They drove back into Jinja and found a hotel overlooking the Gulf at the northern end of Lake Victoria. A bustling market on the same street attracted Margaret's attention. "I think we should buy something for the orphanage," she said.

"What do you suggest?"

"Something they don't have, something they don't grow."

They wandered through the market and decided to buy a large sack of sugar, and two sacks each of wheat and oats. Doug had a young man load the purchases into the back of the Rover, and by the time they returned to the Beyanatha, it was almost dusk. The guard at the gate permitted them to enter and they parked once more in front of the office. The door was locked.

"Now what do we do . . ." Doug mused. "I wonder where Dave has gone."

"Let's take it back to the kitchen. If no one's there, we could just leave the sacks on the counter."

Doug drove slowly past the wash house around to the back where the kitchen lay in shadows. Together they managed to unload their purchases and carried them inside as children's voices sang at twilight. The unfamiliar music drifted across the compound. "We should go over to the hospital and tell one of the nurses what we've done," Margaret said.

"Yes. But we don't want to run into that fellow with the dog."

They walked into the back of the clinic and found a Ugandan aide coming out of the storeroom with a tray of supplies. She looked at them in surprise.

"We were here earlier," Doug explained. "We've just brought some supplies back to the kitchen and wanted to let you know they were there. We intended to see Reverend Davis but the office is locked and he's gone."

"He's here," she said softly. "He comes over every night to be with the children." She led them to the side of the hospital and a porch facing the setting sun.

Doug laid his hand on her arm and raised his finger to his lips. The scene before him was too precious to disturb. There in the dying rays of sunset sat David Davis in a rocking chair, a child wrapped in a blanket across his knee, as the vesper notes lingered on the evening air. Sudden tears came to Doug's eyes and he turned away, taking Margaret's arm to lead her back toward the kitchen. She sensed his spirit was deeply moved and put her arm around his waist to comfort him. He climbed into the car and sat for several moments before turning on the ignition. Shaking his head, he turned to her and said quietly, "And I thought I loved God."

They left Jinja early the next morning and drove along the road skirting the largest lake in Africa, the second largest freshwater lake in the world. High grasses grew abundantly along the roadside with fragments of rain forest in the background. As they crossed into Kenya the area became more populous and they stopped for lunch at a lodge beside Lake Victoria. The fishing fleets on the lake appeared to be from another time period. The white lateen sails stood out vividly against the dark blue water reminding Doug and Margaret of the Arab dhows they had seen at Mombasa. They ordered fillets of the huge Nile Perch which now flourish in the waters of the lake and they found the coarse flesh not unpleasant. The road descended to the south-east and the regional center of Kisumu, a crowded town on the swampy lakeshore where the dreaded parasitic worms are found on snails that cause bilharzia. "So much for swimming in Lake Victoria," Doug mused.

Turning east beyond Kisumu, they headed up into the higher country and the tea capital of Kericho. The emerald green fields stretched for miles along the highway as the road climbed up to the western ridge of the plateau overlooking the Rift Valley. They plunged into shadows as they descended the steep western wall while the sun's rays set on the towering eastern wall across the Valley. It was all ready dark when they pulled up in front of the hotel at Naivasha. Their room was less than ideal but it was all that was available in the midst of the tourist season.

The next morning they discovered a bright blue lake at their doorstep. A pelican sat forlornly on one of a row of fence posts some distance out in the water and they realized the lake level must have risen considerably in recent years. A number of sail boats dotted the lake, and once in awhile a motor boat roared by towing water skiers. "I'm tired," Margaret said. "And this is Sunday, isn't it. Let's call Michael and Dorian and let them know where we are. We can stay here again tonight and go home tomorrow."

Doug laughed as he came back to the table. "Michael was wondering where we had got to. They're coming up for the day."

"From Nairobi?"

"He says it's only an hour away."

Margaret laughed. "Some navigator I am! I thought we were a lot further away than that. It must be this country with all the hills and volcanos and mountains. I don't think I'll ever know exactly where I am!"

Julianne shrieked with delight when she saw her grandparents. "Isn't this a nice idea," Dorian said as she kissed them warmly. "You must tell us what you've been up to since you left home."

"Let's find a place to talk in the shade," Michael suggested. He opened the bag with Julianne's sand toys and Margaret sat in the sand with her as Doug shared their adventures.

"Dad! Are you telling me you beat Arnold Palmer in a golf game!" Michael stared at his father incredulously.

"Yep. I even have the score card to prove it."

Michael frowned as he listened to the fiasco with the car in the mud. "Im glad you didn't run into any hyenas," he said "The Aberdares is no place to be wandering around at any time of the day . . . So, how was your visit to Uganda?"

Margaret raised her eyebrows at Doug's reply. "It's too nice a day to go into all that. I'll tell you another time. Does anybody want to go for a swim?"

Margaret lay down on their bed with Julianne for an afternoon nap while Dorian and Michael and Doug went for a walk on the beach.

"I didn't want to talk about our trip to Uganda in front of Margaret," Doug said quietly. "I'm not sure how she feels about it. In fact, she's barely mentioned it. After we arrived at Beyanatha, David Davis took us on a tour of the place. A little girl had just died and I think that upset Margaret. I saw her touching another poor little thing that looked like she wasn't long for this world either. Margaret's own daughter died of AIDS a couple of years ago."

Michael and Dorian stopped walking and stared at Doug.

"It happened before I met her, but Jane's death has left emotional scars that will never go away. I think Beyanatha has opened up those old wounds. Margaret hasn't mentioned the place since we left. She seems withdrawn and tired."

He shifted his feet. "That David Davis is an awfully fine young man. He's a committed Christian who's chosen to spend his life in the backwaters of Jinja, a place no one's ever heard of, doing a job no one else would want, except me perhaps."

Michael and Dorian stopped again to stare at him.

"The orphanage has a school, and I'm a teacher. When I saw David Davis rocking a little kid to sleep on the porch, something happened inside. I realize I've had a wonderful life, sheltered from the woes of the world for the most part. And now I'm retired and what am I going to do until it's time to meet my Maker. I've been thinking maybe I could lend a hand over here, part-time anyway, just filling in where there's a need."

Michael laid his hand on his father's shoulder. "I don't think it's as simple as all that, Dad. There's visas and work permits and vaccinations . . ."

"I know. But I figure if God wants me to come back to Africa to work, then he'll arrange it somehow. The only thing right now is Margaret. I couldn't come here if it would upset her to be around these dying children. I'll have to wait and see how she feels about it, and I don't think I want to do that just yet."

At that moment, Margaret was lying beside the sleeping child, the rosebud lips slightly parted, her curly hair clinging to her moist skin on her dusky cheeks. Dear little Julianne . . . How fortunate you are to have the protection of a loving father and mother. You'll never end up in a bare hospital room, dying among other sick babies, alone and unloved with nurses who are too busy to hold you and comfort you. She lay her arm lightly across the child. Why did You bring me here, God? And why did I touch that child? I can still feel the bones of that little hand. If I hadn't married Doug, if I had no other commitments, it would be easy to stay in Uganda, to take care of those little ones and just be there to love them. But I can't do that to Doug. I can't tell him I'm sorry I'm his wife because I want to stay at the Haven of Hope for the rest of my life and serve You the way David Davis does. Doug has his home in New Lancaster, his boat, his friends. I can't wrench him away from all that, can I God? I promised to love and honour and cherish him until I die. I can't break a vow I made before You . . . Why do I feel this burden, God? Is it because of Jane? Because I didn't take care of her the way I should have when she was dying? Is this to salve my guilty conscience? Or is it a genuine call on my life to serve You here? Oh God! I don't know what I'm doing! If I'm to have any peace of mind about this I'll have to forget what happened to me there. That's what I'll do . . . I'll put it out of my mind. If that's possible . . .

When Julianne woke up, Margaret took her out to the veranda. The lake shimmered under a bright white sky. Doug and Dorian and Michael were sitting under a thatched roof near a grove of oleanders and hibiscus. She led the little girl toward them, a smile on her face and saying gaily, "Here's Grampa. Do you think he'll buy us an ice-cream cone?"

She made an effort to be cheerful and light-spirited for the rest of the afternoon. As the family left to return to Nairobi before sundown, she kissed them happily and said she was looking forward to seeing them the next day. And when she and Doug went to bed that night she made love to him with an intensity that surprised him and made him suspicious that all her gaiety was a charade, masquerading a deep unhappiness, an unresolved grief buried deep in her heart.

They returned to Nairobi and the sparkling clean house after lunch. Lulu had put Julianne down for a nap, Mwangi was polishing the wooden floor on his hands and knees. They unpacked their bags and sat on the veranda at the back of the house, reading and dozing and dreaming of their latest adventures.

They were scheduled to leave Friday at noon to return to Rome, and spent the last days in Kenya, shopping, touring the university and cultural center. Doug played nine holes of golf one afternoon with Michael and laughed as he came home to tell Margaret that some of the golf courses in Kenya had a rule that if your ball dropped beside a hippopotamus or a crocodile, you could drop another ball at a safe distance with no penalty.

Margaret and Julianne had gone for a walk that morning and stopped to watch a lawn bowling tournament for a few minutes. "I wonder if the same rules apply for lawn bowling as golf," she said. "I noticed many of the players were accompanied by their dogs, wolf-hounds, setters and German shepherds. Surely they wouldn't expect their dog to protect them from a crocodile."

"You won't find crocodiles in Nairobi, Margaret," Michael said. "The people are more likely to need protection from pick-pockets, purse-snatchers and petty thieves. There's been an increase in that kind of crime as more and more young people come into the city and can't find work."

"I've noticed them too," Doug said. "When we first got here, we were so overwhelmed by the sights that I didn't notice the people. Now

I can see this country has a severe problem with unemployment. There are so many people wandering about with nothing to do."

Michael nodded. "It's the population increase. The birth rate is going up, or rather the death rate is going down. Infant mortality is away down now. Like I said before, a Kenyan woman will average eight living children, but the educational system can only afford one of them."

"Is that true?" Margaret asked. "I've seen any number of girls and boys in their different school uniforms. They looked so smart in their white blouses and coloured skirts and pants."

Michael nodded his head again. "But you haven't seen the ghettoes of Nairobi and Mombasa. And we never saw the pockets of poverty in the country. I wouldn't want to take you anywhere near those."

"And what about AIDS?" she asked.

Michael glanced at his father. "That's another story too. The World Health Organization holds conferences each year and it's always bad news. AIDS is rampant among the tribal peoples of equatorial Africa. The Muslims to the north are affected to a lesser degree because of the Islamic laws. There's some success with the educational programs on the west coast but unless a cure or a vaccine is found soon, the medical resources we have now will never be able to cope with the problem. One day, all the millions who are infected with the virus now, will be literally dying in the streets. If and when that happens, I may just turn tail and run for home."

Doug cleared his throat. "Michael was hoping we'd run into Arnold Palmer and his buddies on the golf course this afternoon. The tournament is starting next week and he thought they might be out to check the course. I'm relieved though. He might have wanted to play a revenge match, and I could never live up to my reputation."

Friday morning they said their goodbyes to Dorian and Julianne, and Lulu and Mwangi. Sudden tears sprang to Margaret's eyes as she hugged her daughter-in-law and grandchild for the last time. "Isn't this silly!" she wiped her eyes. "You'd think we were going to the moon. And we'll see you later this spring or summer. You will come to New Lancaster, won't you."

Dorian wiped her eyes too. "I guess I can handle New Lancaster as long as you and Doug are there. I'll let you know what's happening with Atlanta."

Michael drove them to the airport, parked near the front door and arranged for their luggage. He hugged his father tightly for a long time, and then turned to Margaret. He hugged her too with tears in his eyes. "I'm so glad that Dad has you. And we'll see you soon at home."

She smiled brightly through more tears. "We'll be waiting for you, dear. We'll dust your old room and Julianne and Dorian will grow to love New Lancaster as much as I do."

The silver-winged Alitalia flight soared off the runway into the winds blowing up the plateau from Mombasa, banked to the left, heading north as Doug and Margaret gazed silently out the window at the expanse of the city in the midst of the tawny green grasses of the veldt. Before they climbed into the white sky they saw Mount Kenya's pink snow cap in the distance, the dark forests to the west and Mount Elgon on the western horizon. Doug turned Margaret's hand over in his and sighed.

She glanced at him.

"Well that's Kenya," he said. "Now for Italy."

The End. to be continued